Also by Daniel R. Connelly

Extravagant Stranger (Little Island Press/Carcanet, 2017)

Donkey See, Donkey Do (Eyewear, 2017)

THE INCONTINENT OF ROYY

Daniel R. Connelly

ISBN: 978-1-915079-19-0

Cover design by Aaron Kent

Edited & Typeset by Aaron Kent

Broken Sleep Books (2022)

Broken Sleep Books Ltd
Rhydwen,
Talgarreg,
SA44 4HB
Wales

Contents

The Incontinent of Royy

Daniel R. Connelly

We degrade Providence too much by attributing our ideas to it out of annoyance at being unable to understand it.
— Fyodor Dostoyevsky, 'The Idiot'

I am interested only in "nonsense"; only in that which makes no practical sense. I am interested in life only in its absurd manifestations.
— Daniil Kharms, 'Today I wrote nothing'

I spent quite a while gazing out and pondering what primeval forces had conspired together to create such a place. Then I ate my sandwiches.
— Magnus Mills, 'Only When the Sun Shines Brightly'

For my son, Florian
Per Aspera Ad Astra

Prologue – Bang!

There was a Bang! but nobody heard it. The universe shattered but there was nobody there to see. It was tremendous. There were holes everywhere. The sky wasn't yet. There was a lot of gas. It's all so impossible to imagine let alone find the right words for. Planet earth was carved from chaos. It's been in the blood for four billion years. Continents split from the main until there was no main, rivers sprang, mountains erupted through rock, eco systems were born because weather. *Terra firma*, cluelessness, what's happening? Chaos, that's what. The dinosaurs had chaos down. I've seen the movies.

Chaos was in the bones of the first fish to walk out of the sea, it was all very nonchalant, like 'it's just me so I'll boss the joint'. But there was no joint to boss until others came in their own good time, flapped around until they had legs, stood up, pointed at something, gave it a one-syllable name. Soon after came a lot of anguish over who had the safest cave, which led to unspeakable violence. Vegetables began to grow. They changed the landscape. There were broccoli spears. Lots of men and women were fucking because it felt good. Clothing became necessary. Then more clothing as their children grew. Soon after came a lot of anguish over who had the sickest gear, which lead to unspeakable violence, and fashion.

Sun worship became necessary because life was tough and questions needed answering. Leaders rose to conduct the services; it was all very holier-than-thou. Groups formed when the priests alternately picked their favourites until it was just the dying guy at the end. They all waited until the dying guy was dead and missed him. They put a huge rock on top of his body and went their way.

Picture these cavepeople. Little heads with loping jaws. Wayward gaits. Tense fists. Intimacy was brutal. Loin cloths with crude decorations but at least something. It was a start. Faces up to the sky looking for the sun in the rain. Getting soaked. Early forms of pneumonia. More missing. More huge rocks. Bear-skinned in the glare of day, men and women picked things from the ground, had a quick bite, see if it was heading cave-wards. Some of it was rock hard and fit neatly in the palm. Exchanges of weapons. Practice on each other. Impulse control issues. Casual slaughter. Missing. Rocks. The spoils of chaos. Jealousy. Covetousness. The first side-eye. Lots of loiterers around cave entrances. The general lack of trust.

We had a vague idea of who we were, we addressed one another crudely, fair enough, it was all a very long time ago and anyway consciousness doesn't mean conscience so chaos was always close to the surface, likely to break out over the smallest of misunderstandings, like 'there wasn't enough wood for the fire' or 'it was your turn to kill the bears' or 'what are you looking at?' Rage won every day. But there was fucking every night, the desire to spread the seed a very long way down time. There were bangs and everybody heard them.

Abubelle

Observing a single day on the continent of Royy is, like a high-topped couture boot, laced with difficulty. Second-by-second social interactions grip our millions of citizens; threads of serendipity splice in the blink of an eye across our wide stretch of land, which unfurls like a tongue in a sauna, from lake to mountain, beach to forest, the climates from hot to cold and several points between. The weather can be appalling. We try to be hardy but fail. We're not the friendliest. In pettiness and violence we excel. Luckily, root vegetables are in abundance. It had been on my mind for years to take in the workings of our continent synchronically, a snapshot of time from the book of wonders I house within my comfortable existence. In short, I was after the chance to take to the skies, and once and for all look down on the men and women of Royy.

Imagine my joy when I found myself drinking with my light-aircraft-pilot friend, Ohnoo. After chatting old times when I reminded him of the photos, Ohnoo soon offered me an option to see Royy from above. It's a twin-seater, said Ohnoo, we'll need to refuel, get some decent sounds going, strap back and levitate, but I reckon we can see all Royy in the space of 24 hours. Even in the dark, Ohnoo, I said. Yes, Abubelle, he replied, that's when the fires burn brightest. When's best for you, I said, in the usual polite and undemanding manner. Any time you're ready, Abubelle, said Ohnoo, Killer Queen, my Cessna 9587dash2 is fuelled up in the car park. I made for the window because Ohnoo had drunk seven but there she was, Killer Queen, a rare aeronautical beauty amid the tired saloon cars out back.

I turned and watched Ohnoo slam his glass down on the counter and demand number eight from Dermotich the Publican. Ohnoo loves drinking whereas I'm a lightweight, only last week I dropped in on Yardburger and helped her demolish a bottle of whisky. I say help, I had a smidgeon. I say demolish, she licked the rim dry. Her skin changed colour. I spend a lot of my life surrounded by drinkers. I see a lot of skin change colour.

Come on then Ohnoo, I said, slapping his shoulders, fly me over the scalp of Royy. Show me the topsoil of our continent's daily life. Give us both a panorama to remember. Ohnoo looked at me with one eye closed, slammed his glass down, one for the air, Dermotich, he said, and leant into the wooden structure at an awkward angle. When she was sure Ohnoo wasn't watching, Dermotich shook her head. I think she wanted my attention but I was buzzing. This was the shit. I was living the dream, about to cross transnational boundaries which from 20,000 feet disappear into thin air, it's a mess of ordinance survey; anything could happen.

And for every time that truism comes true, anything did. After his fourth one for the air, Ohnoo fell from his stool and splayed on the sawdusted floor. He purged an enormous amount of liquid from his mouth. Its range was impressive. The sawdust got straight to work. There was a gash in Ohnoo's head so Dermotich came round and didn't like what she saw. That's a lot of liquid, she said, and phoned for an ambulance.

Ohnoo is still in hospital. They found several cancers. He is caught in a web of wires. I visited him. I told him how disappointed I was that his habits spoiled my dream of looking down on all Royy. He said, I'm going to be dead this time next week, Abubelle, and I said nothing but I was thinking my aerial scoop is out the window and not coming my way again any time soon, you've brought this on yourself, Ohnoo, it's no way to go around being. I then smiled easily and looked at him with my tender eyes. I attended his funeral in a pilot's suit. I wanted people to know. Killer Queen is still in the car park. Dermotich is sawing it up at the weekend.

Tele

I'm walking back from the market with a bag of beetroot. They are the colour of congealed blood and hard as truncheons. I don't want things to kick off and be without them. It's the rough part of town. Scarsenegaat, the loiterer, gave me her sideways look which stretched from Hild the Florist's all the way down to Excelunt the Couturier's. Something was brewing in the ale house and I wanted to be in charge of the gas canisters. What's Koppleler doing in a sleeping bag snug against the station entrance? I'm down on my luck, he replied. Two trains bombed through, the masonry shook, a pigeon – an Antwerp Smerle I believe – flew out of the exposed rafters followed by her children. Invention abuts nature, I said to Kopplerer, feeling in my pocket for a coin. The last time I saw you you'd received a small grant from the state towards your artistic enterprises, now this! which was intended to be a question but came out wrong.

Let me tell you, Tele, I'll tell you, said Kopplerer, his face poking through the bag's open end. He was the shadow of a babushka doll. I think he was fucking with my name. I staked all on poetry, he said, when I'd have been better off writing crime fiction, particularly here in Royy where there's no end to the exciting plot-driven lives of millions. He looked mournful, like a priest on Good Friday. Oh, Tele, he said, and hauled himself up against the wall as another pair of trains rocketed through and some dust landed inside Kopplerer's centre parting. By every measure, he said, I am worthless. We all have rough times, Kopplerer, I said, looking forward to a hot dinner and a comfortable bed. This too will pass, I said, wafting my arms around the vicinity. I reached for the most direct way to explain what it is to be, said Kopplerer, and I sold seven copies, and three of those wanted their money back. They are related to me. I cannot begin to tell you, he said, which I found odd because I thought he'd finished telling me.

They said of my debut collection, he said, painstakingly put together in the time the small grant bought, that I'd 'tried to sneak into first class with coach class cognisance', that my poetry sat on the line like a 'shit biscuit', and from Wetheart at *The Daily Courier* that if this was poetry she was a cow, which was most unkind given what she told me about her birthday last month. I knew I had the right words but they came out in the wrong order, Kopplerer said. The publisher cut ties. I had ruined his summer, he said. My wife threw me out. She was embarrassed by my futility, she said, and handed me the sleeping bag. It's noisy here and people couldn't care less. It's perfect. I was surprised to see the Antwerp Smerle, I thought she'd died.

And if you could do it again, Kopplerer, I said, how would your route differ? He looked at me as if I was talking nonsense, as if my figure of speech had misfired. Kopplerer knows all about misfiring, he can't write for shit, I thought to myself eyeballing him. If I get you right, said Kopplerer, removing an arm from inside the bag, you're asking me what exactly? Oh, I said, do you have a novel in you? Yes, said Kopplerer, and now I think that's exactly where it should stay. I flipped him 2 Bits and he caught them cleanly. There's no money in writing, Tele, he said, nodding at his bounty. There's only other people's money in your writing I said before I could stop myself, and you've fucked that up, poet, I said. This is an annoying habit I have developed. My mother was first to mention it. I told her to get lost.

Kopplerer looked shocked. I should have gone for murder mystery, he said, instead of trying to encapsulate the entire human condition. I thought he said conditioner and glanced at his sorry hair. Is there nobody you can turn to in this time of need, I said, waving to Dubbsey who dashed into the ticket office. He owes me. My words struck all the wrong chords, said Kopplerer, too indulgently for my liking. I am a one-star writer forever more, he said, and burst into tears which I found embarrassing. Commuters might think it was my doing. I have read the reviews, his poetry is bilge. I didn't know where to look so I looked at my feet. There was an iridescent caterpillar mounting my new trainer. It felt like a metaphor.

Eyeroid

It was one of the great days of the year. The streets were awash with flags and Eglott the Bunting Seller was smoking a long cigar, having freshly sold out of his festive *crepe* tendrils. Crowds gathered early to get the best roadside view. The finishing post was alive in neon, and a local band – The Geoffreydots! – were warming up on a small stage in the winners' reception area. One of the great days of the year, when schools close and children throng, some are held up or are sat on their fathers' shoulders for a better view, a day to remember for the rest of their lives. One dad, Dŭnk, put his son back down on the ground through sheer envy. Dŭnk had struggled recently with self-esteem issues. His boy was devastated. Everywhere else the street looked marvellous, alive, celebratory. The swishing cyclists would be met, as every year, with nothing short of frenzy.

Three hundred riders from all corners of Royy had descended on the town with their racing bicycles. The engineering was superlative and the cost-per-bike inestimable. The restaurants were rammed. Lined up outside 'Rookle, the Ironmongers', in their silver vests and stretchy shorts, the riders resembled a mercury flow. The annual all-comers five-mile dash would have the appearance of an electric eel. Dill had won the previous four dashes and was red hot favourite to storm to another victory. She wore a pink rose on her lightning-strike of a helmet to remember her mother who had recently died. Dill didn't feel sad but she did feel dutiful.

The race officials were readying for the whistle. But wait, said Onlong, the event director, one rider has failed to arrive. She checked her sponsored clipboard, looked around and said, has anyone seen Eyeroid? With the riders straining their wiry muscles – frankly, they're trained to race, not to hang around waiting for no-shows – who should come round the corner but Eyeroid himself, sat square on an orange tricycle, beeping the novelty horn. Everyone cracked up, including the seriously competitive riders; the crowd pointed at Eyeroid on three wheels and gales of laughter blew on the breeze. The Geoffreydots! struck up their version of Loser by the super-famous singer, Feck. All around the ground shook with mirth and solid beats. Sorry I'm late, said Eyeroid, I was just adjusting the basket on the back. The howls of laughter eventually abated because everyone knew it was right now that a shit-hot, once-a-year race needed to get under way. And did it get under way?

The claxon blared like in wartime and the mercury flow shot into the distance to climb the nearside of Birdberry Hill. The backs of the zooming pack flashed under the sun and the sight was almost science fiction. Instantly alone, Eyeroid pedalled majestically, waving his hands – at times both of them were off the handlebars – and gathered pace as he conquered the first twenty yards. There were still plenty of smiles but the locals had laughed enough for one day, someone said.

What no-one knew is that Eyeroid was in truth late because he'd spread a slick of oil from his basket one side of the road to the other at the bottom of Birdberry Hill. Eyeroid had never had any scruples and this year he decided to act upon their absence. What came next was unaccountably brutal. I have the words for it but I don't feel comfortable using them. I'll do my best.

There was a blood river of crushed machines, their pilots eviscerated, it was more like a scrapyard than anything else, one with innards and punctured flesh to complement the sharded mass of titanium alloy and twisted aluminium. The scene recalled the worst excesses of the Hodgson/Oyuunchimeg dispute, still so fresh in people's minds. Several riders were spread-eagled on the tarmacadam, barely breathing, the champion, Dill, her pink rose crushed, her tender heart penetrated by spoke upon spoke, died in someone's arms, while others called for help with their broken mouths.

Fatalities were quickly mounting when Eyeroid freewheeled down to the bottom, pulled on his brakes and swerved, albeit slowly, his legs were not lithe and strong, around the hellish heap, and on he went, pedalling puffingly up the hill in the second of his two gears. As he rounded the crest into town in a time of one hour five minutes and eight seconds, or, as Ylom the Dentist incorrectly shouted out when Eyeroid tootled past, a shade under 10 minutes per mile, Eyeroid heard from far behind him the anguished death rattle of a croaking competitor. The Geoffreydots! struck up Royy's national anthem and the teary-eyed spectators felt rotten that they had so openly mocked a man on three wheels.

Eyeroid was instead greeted with a rapture close to the pure love a mother has for her newborn. He'd ultimately swayed the crowd with his delightful approach and earnest manner. He beeped the novelty horn repeatedly and collected the prize of a bullock painted silver for the day. He then spoke to the many interviewers who had appeared from all walks of town life.

On the way home Eyeroid stopped off at the bottom of Birdberry Hill, leant his orange tricycle carefully against a sturdy bush, and knelt down to commiserate with the mangled mass. What a freak occurrence, he said to the many bodies skewered into the ground, it must have been a tractor from Brethelkopf's farm, I'm sure the ambulances will be here soon. But Eyeroid lied and he knew it. He rode clean away and he'd clean lied. Not only had he himself laid down the deadly slick which took the lives of dozens of innocents on a sporting day out in the sun, but he had cut the telephone lines to the local hospital. It was no freak occurrence, there was completely nothing doing. Why it was that Eyeroid chose this particular year to announce himself as a town legend we will probably never know. In everyone a grenade, I suppose. Honestly, tricopaths …

Woolff

Smil took early retirement from the toy factory, it was time to surround himself with good-looking younger people in a relaxed environment before he dropped down dead. He had a pension coming, appropriate to thirty years stuffing teddies, rabbits, snakes, lions and unicorns. I bought one for my daughter, it fell apart and so did she. There was also the sum left in his father's will. Smil had been a dutiful son who lied to save himself when necessary, and his father's generosity and sheer ignorance saw enough to fund a small apartment by a lake which had become the stuff of Smil's dreams, he would lie in, pleasure himself and take late coffee.

On his way back from an early jaunt to the supermarket next to Toga's Lighting Emporium, Smil dashed across the road to a bright advertising hoarding bearing a glowing couple with their curly blond child outside a four-story apartment block backing onto a lake. Everything glistened and gleamed. He couldn't take his eyes off their teeth. These are my people, thought Smil, and he pulled a broken pencil from his back pocket and a waiter's notepad he carried for all his ideas. He wrote down the telephone number and within hours Smil had changed into a t-shirt and trainers and was sat on a swivel chair in the trendy office of Woolff, the estate agent.

I want to buy an apartment with a clear view of the lake, Smil said, and I want to be surrounded by these people, he said, gesturing towards the smaller, brochure size advertisement propped up on the desk in front of him. Oh they're a charming family, said Woolff, it has a young vibe, the condo, lots of creatives, she said, taking in Smil's t-shirt and trainers. The young couple and son radiate joy, said Smil, it's no wonder I've fallen for them, they looked blessed with happiness, love and hygiene, the kid on his dad's shoulders, mum to the side beaming into the camera, palpable freedom in tandem with sensible family responsibility, said Smil out loud and the estate agent's mouth fell open slowly and she closed her left eye. I want a viewing, now, said Smil, and he wrote something down. The estate agent closed her mouth, opened her left eye, stood up and went for the door, opened her mouth again and said, I'll drive you there.

They were crossing to the lake side of town in Woolff's spacious six-door when Smil turned to her and said, I'd like to meet that family while we're there. Family, said Woolff? Yes, all three of them, said Smil. They look delightful. I'd like to drop in an early hello to my new neighbours, he said, holding the brochure up, but Woolff's eyes were on the road and her heart began to quicken. She looked long into the rear-view mirror at the desolate streets behind and thought, doesn't he know they're not real, is he not aware they've never actually met before the photo shoot and none of them speaks the same language. Woolff's head stuttered under the weight of it. I need to pull over, she said, make a phone call.

Woolff returned calmer. She whipped a fishcake and fork out of her jacket and ate before getting back into her executive van. Half an hour's drive through the diseased traffic later, Woolff turned into a gated entrance with a waxwork policeman stood up inside a security booth. Woolff waved and drove through. They alighted at the end of the gravel and the apartments stood tall in the sun like something bleached and biblical. The perfect couple were waiting on an immaculately small lawn of Bahia grass, they weren't holding hands but they were looking around as if for answers. Where is your beautiful son, said Smil, I thought he would be joining us, you look younger in the photo, and your wife, hello, I'm Smil, and you are? he said. I am ... I am Devon, she said, my husband is there with his hood up, she said, pointing to him though she could equally have reached out and touched his shoulder gently. Hello, said the husband, my name is, er, Pullit, he said, tugging on his hoody. Smil wrote something down. And your son, where is your young son with the beautiful blond curls said Smil, and at exactly the same time, like they were a famous duet, Devon said Oh, you mean Loftus and Pullit said Oh, you mean Sten, which was embarrassing for them.

He has several names, said Devon, sharply, but the one we use most is Sten. I've always preferred Loftus, said Pullit, getting into the game. Devon laughed lightly and her hair moved awkwardly like it had dislocated itself and Pullit and Smil were amazed like children in front of a burning barn. Are you wearing a wig, said Smil? No it's not a wig it's my head, they are investigating. Yes, said Pullit, it's a wig, she's got cancer, and Devon's eyes bulged. Cancer since the original photo said Smil? That's right, said Devon, and a funny head as well. It was difficult being the perfect family, said Pullit, a number of things cascaded at once. We were very nearly broken by the cancer, and my head, said Devon, yes, your head, said Pullit. But I'm still me, Devon said. Still me too, said Pullit, zipping the hoody up tight. Smil wrote something down.

They said their goodbyes and dashed back inside the whitewashed condo to look for Loftus or Sten, because we all take a long nap about now. Questions were gathering slowly in Woolff's mind and she started sweating again, the ambience around her armpits was reprehensible. Well, they may not be the same as they were when they beamed out of the picture at me, said Smil putting an arm on Woolff's shoulder, it quivered, but I like them the more for it, said Smil, they've lost a bit of glamour, yes. Lost their son as well, said Woolff quickly and winced as soon as it was out. I mean he's probably playing with his cars, said Woolff, yes, said Smil, and I bet he's got an animal stuffed by these very hands, he said, crossing them behind his back before whipping out his waiter's pad and signing the cheque he'd written with a pencil while Woolff burst into floods of tears which turned to joy in no time at all.

Stillañak

Although he once possessed many fine qualities, Stillañak will forever be known as the driver of the laundry van that knocked down Royy's most famous philosopher, Denkstit, a global expert on signs taken for wonders, right outside the royal palace which they were both leaving, the philosopher with a gold medal, Stillañak with soiled shirts.

The philosopher's head was in the clouds after the modest lunch at his request, just he and the popular, literature-loving president bonding over soup and *baguettes*, perhaps Denkstit was contemplating his medal as a simulacrum or a sign of conscious reactionary conformity when Stillañak turned the corner carefully, obeying all lights, and wallop, philosopher bonnet, bonnet philosopher, brake, slide, stone dead, dead as many of the greats who had carried him on their shoulders, ancient and modern. Denkstit was a national treasure and no-one knew why. But people are ready to blame and our gods judge harshly.

Folk can be so nasty, so unnecessary. Immediately his identity broke and TV crews pitched up at his bungalow which was disturbing for his wife and children, no-one saw Stillañak the way he was anymore, no longer was he Stillañak-the-laundry-guy to his friends at the bar but a symbol of teleological capitalist global-warming denial; to his parents a heart-breaking indictment of the collapse of standards in contemporary western society; or simply a loose cannon behind the wheel.

Stillañak faced no judicial punishment for the philosopher's death. He was blameless, his eyesight tested, tested again, and fine, the philosopher's family should, indeed, be grateful Stillañak was at the wheel, given his lengthy experience of transporting dirty and/or clean laundry, or there'd be nothing left to stick in a coffin, funded by the state, shaped like a question mark, and of the highest order.

Sadly, Denkstit's death was only the beginning. All life went awry. It was the merest consolation but Stillañak, who mostly stayed home, went on to read the complete works of his road-kill, eventually going out of his mind wondering what the philosopher of signs taken for wonders would have written about his own means of death, there's probably a multi-chaptered publication Denkstit's missed out on there, repeated poor Stillañak over and over to himself, banging his head against a cushioned wall, and there are others out there like him in Royy, all mad.

Warblers

The shop had remained the same for decades, the only difference being where Old Warbler once climbed the wooden stepladder, these days Otto took care of the high stacking of bird whistles. Their fame cannot be over-celebrated. Old Warbler & Son had for fifty years commanded the interest of the grandmasters of birdsong who thronged to the *Warbler Shrine of Chirp* in the city's deep south in order to play and purchase sweet airy sounds till they had taken their fill. Notwithstanding recent imports from China, a Warbler whistle remained the *ne plus ultra* of champion chirrupers.

The premises, perhaps the size of a small coach house, were filled wall-to-wall, shelf-upon-shelf, with boxed bird-whistles. Radically, when Otto took overall command of the steps, he re-arranged the boxes at floor level to house the deep whistles, such as that of the Common Raven or the downslurring Northern Cardinal, then moved up in space and pitch until on tiptoe at the top of the steps he placed the boxes containing the Tufted Titmouse and the Pacific-slope Flycatcher and the nip of the black-headed Grosbeak. The middle shelves were filled with less clear-cut pitches like that of the Bullock's Oriole or the Hermit Thrush or Say's Phoebe's-burr which sounds to me like a complaint. The shop was always full of jacketed men putting whistles to their lips and filling the tiny room with nature's orchestra. Sometimes, though, it all sounded like a warming up of instruments, it could and often did get a bit lary.

One afternoon, an enthusiast presented herself for the first time to Old Warbler & Son. To say she was beautiful is almost pointless. Father, son and every jacketed client turned as one, whistles in mouths, as a slip of shimmering elegance and grace moved from the entrance to the counter, behind which sat Old Warbler next to the cash register. Her perfume was perfect. Otto's ladder wobbled. Not a fake bird sounded. She might have been thirty, it really didn't matter.

Leaning over the counter she asked Old Warbler whether he had a Red-Breasted Nuthatch and for the first time in his life he was unable to answer. He just sat there gawping. Looking up to Otto, she said is that where you keep the Great-Horned Owl then, and Otto's ladder shook again but like his dad he was silent, even though all had lit up in the forest of their minds.

The jacketed customers let loose a brief ripple, more a fugue of trill, but inadvertently. She was so intoxicating, so mesmeric, the clients fell into a human tableau, not a muscle moving, a roomful of mannequins around whom the arriviste sidled like a Siamese cat coming to realise its full potential in the world.

She breezed here and there until spotting what she'd been looking for all along in the mouth of a statue in a jacket by the door: an Old Warbler & Son Northern Mockingbird. She removed it from the dummy's mouth, wiped it with a Wet One from her Gucci bag, re-boxed it, popped it back, fastened the expensive clasp and walked clean out of the store, not any store, but the world-famous-for-bird-whistles Old Warbler & Son which at that moment contained figurines as if in a tourist castle somewhere, male enthusiasts of birdsong stood shock still; for the first time in 50 years the room was filled with silence.

Outside, trailing away into the late afternoon, she blew strains of the Northern Mockingbird. She'd tossed out the Nuthatch and Owl requests on the spur of the moment and was inwardly astonished at their resonance, there was a huge surge of power. She didn't need to reveal her true desire nor her own name. To think this never happened before Otto took control of the steps.

Angela

Sister Angela was caught in a fierce gale on the corner of the High Street with Erms the Fishmonger on one side and Van der Hunk the Butcher on the other. The squalor mixed up their smells something rotten. Her habit was in turmoil so I dashed across to her, though quite what I could do had to be up in the air. It was as windy as I can ever remember it, wind like this is the revenge of the gods I thought to myself but I had read Shakespeare late into last night.

I was acutely aware of the potential pitfalls of this sudden sorry state of affairs but as a man who appreciates not only rarefied literature but also people of faith, I was keen to help the distressed sister. It felt like I was driven towards her. Miserably, when I got to the nun I'd known for a month her crucifix had already been ripped clean away while her scapular was dancing down the road. Sister Angela shouted and shouted until her veil took off vertically to reveal a hole where her face should be. I was astonished like a cow under the knife and there was no reply to my single question.

Another great squall of wind took her gown away and then the whole lot came off in what was now a full-blown theological cyclone, even her two underskirts and soon there was a perfect Sister Angela-shaped gap which I stepped through in my tracksuit on the way to buy some filters from Colaba the Tobacconist tobacco shop whose awning was hanging half off, banging in the gale like the proverbial shit-house door. I'd never have guessed there were two underskirts, both black, what's that all about?

Järvinen

As arranged, I met Hämäläinen in the sauna after work. He nodded as I entered before breaking into a sort of smile because I had thought to bring him a cold beer. There followed a period of intense silence during which we drank our beer and stared at the stove. Occasionally, Hämäläinen would get up to pour water on the stones, at other times he spoke, saying, it's your turn now, Järvinen. After 30 minutes I felt that Hämäläinen was getting ready to say something substantial, he looked at me, and away, and at me again with his rock-solid, below-zero face. A slight tension rose as sweat poured down us like something I can't explain.

Järvinen, he began, I don't know if I've ever told you, but I have a daughter with the mayor's wife. This was hard enough to consider and compounded by the fact that right at that very moment who should walk in flinging his towel to one side if not Jackson, the mayor. I had no idea of the enmity that lay between them, but it became obvious when the first thing Hämäläinen said was, Jackson, I fucked your wife like a pig last night where were you?

Now look here, said Jackson, I'll not put up with personal abuse during sauna-time. I have come to think away from my current woes, or perhaps to confront them in a more conducive environment of tranquillity, steam, and massive introspection, all clearly currently unavailable except steam. At this he hit Hämäläinen over the head with the ladle. Hämäläinen responded by smashing his bottle of beer into Jackson's face, which made him stumble, fall briefly onto the stove where his flesh sizzled, and drop dead on the planked floor; an extraordinary sight, I must say, naked men damaging one another for old time's sakes in a sauna leading directly to a manslaughter.

Again, there ensued a period of intense silence while we looked at the body, Jackson's profuse blood beginning to fry. Järvinen, I haven't been to a funeral in ten years, said Hämäläinen, out of the blue. I've been closer to my own than any other. Besides, mayors' wives have the worst reputation for fucking in all Royy and from what I hear my daughter won't miss him much either, he said, climbing over Jackson's steaming corpse on the way to bring us another beer.

Matunga

Next to me at the traffic lights in a convertible was a smiling Obedele. I wound my window down by hand. What are you so happy about, smiling, Obedele? I asked. Everything, Matunga, everything! exclaimed Obedele; finally, I don't have any friends! At this, he lit a long cigar. I've had successful fallings out with you, you bitch, and with Kharms, Smithson, Njere, Monstserrat and Idi, bitches or sons or daughters of bitches one and all. I feel so unburdened, he said. What is it about you and people, I asked him? Just then the lights changed and the convertible behind Obedele beeped its horn. Obedele put on his handbrake, car into neutral, undid his seatbelt, opened the door – by this time many horns were blowing - walked to the car behind, clenched his fist, and banged the driver right on top of the head. He slumped immediately down onto his steering wheel, stone dead.

And that's really all that happened at those traffic lights. Oh, and all the horns stopped at once.

Hatzumake

Every year, about a month before high school exams, Xavier hired a theatre in the centre of town and performed a limited run of his one-man re-telling of the notoriously difficult 18th-century novel assigned by the exam board every year. The other eleven months he spent following Royy's various cricket teams around the world, staying in some sick hotels.

The novel was about marriage chasers and posh living but the language was as thick as tarmacadam and the students didn't have time for that shit. Cue: a top-hat, cloak, thigh-high boots, a flyweight white shirt and lots of make-up which transported Xavier not only spiritually but also geographically, which he liked. Students who had not bothered to read the text poured in sure as spikes on a gate to see the show, during which Xavier launched himself alone into the strict courtier's mores; mannered and protracted, he threw his arms around every night just like a juggler his sticks. It is an incredibly boring novel but a national treasure. The show was average but necessary.

Of the many thousands of students who'd attended down the years, one, Hatzumake, became so entranced by this sole presence on stage giving a performance that was almost the same every night, twice on Wednesdays, that she found herself stealing from her mother's purse to go the next night; and the next; and again; after which she told her mother and her mother was very happy with her daughter's honesty and sudden theatrical interest, for she herself had been an actress once and had often wondered whether her daughter might follow in her steps, as it were. Instead, selfless Hatzumake had gone into dentistry to help with her family's disastrous teeth; and the next; and the matinee; and the one after.

Hatzumake became well known by the staff at the theatre and had met Xavier personally when he sat her on his knee during an intermission some time ago. She was staggered every time; the man was lightning at his job; full houses for four weeks of the year and then off to wallop the cricketing foes.

In short, for the previous fifty years Hatzumake had gone to every performance, the one month of the year before exams, for the chance to see Xavier bring forth his unbending blend of historic histrionic narrator who quick-changes into each shadow and basically lays out everyone's reason for being there, like a classy Spark Notes but in three dimensions. The house lights were on throughout so the audience could write stuff down.

By now in his eighties, with thousands of performances behind him, never needing to work again having cracked it as the noble participant/observer, Xavier snapped one night before he went on stage. He is only a man after all, but one who has made a lot of money pretending to be someone else, like a criminal would do. He cannot and will not play the role that night nor likely ever again, he told the manager, even if it only is one month-a-year, same as ever, fifty or so shows all in then cab it to the airport.

I'll swap it all for an allotment! he shouted, our cricket teams are shit, they never win, and I am getting old, fat and lazy in front of strangers. Enough! Xavier cried as the five-minute bell rang in the Bauhaus-style lobby which was full of teenagers on their phones talking about food. I'll not leave this Green Room tonight, he said having calmed a little, from behind the locked-door.

A hastily-convened meeting of the management decided to offer Hatzumake the role, for tonight at least. She was their theatre, she'd seen every show performed in the last half century, she'll know the words. And she said Yes when they asked her and before you can say whodunnit Hatzumake was dressed as a nobleman while Xavier sat in his underwear, door wide open, lock smashed.

He heard a kind of performance he could never have imagined; one of pauses and ellipses, even moments of complete silence. Here was a different protagonist indeed, one with an eye on the new to bring in even more students, yet steeped in theatrical history having watched Xavier every day, all her life. Hatzumake was also an autodidact, and as such, an avid exponent of the nation's post-war theatrical manifestos; a lurch towards the unknown, the unanswerable, and the plainly absurd.

Hatzumake brewed under lights. After three or four performances, theatre directors from across Royy jetted in to see the newcomer's nightly refutation of Xavier's craft, bombast and screecher that he was. Here instead, they all agreed, was a major shift in the lie of the stage, like when Shakespeare picked up the ball and ran with it back in the day.

Xavier despised her success, it was as if generations had turned their backs on him all at the same time, front-row members he recalls in pretty bows or more recent, sharp-lined haircuts, beautiful breasts, equally panicking before exam day; they had all turned away, they were gone. He flew to the South to watch Royy lose and died of a drug overdose in his hired car; there was a service.

Hatzumake had the world at her feet, because she had somehow, with no acting skill whatsoever, stumbled onto a new approach to the stage. There was ambiguity in 18th-century glances. There were questions followed by long silences. There was overlapping dialogue, impressive for a one-woman show.

As a theatre-going critic sat among a thousand teens on their phones I have to say Hatzumake's change of direction has shoved theatre off its tracks. I am made to feel uncomfortable by her oppressive silences and seeming loss of concentration, which gets me wondering whether ... but then what if ... and then feeling stupid when obviously they hadn't ... What a professional!

Wickramasinghe

The school backs right onto the street and with the windows open on a hot afternoon, I could see Blake, Gish, Wijedije, Fernandy, Dill, Zimmer, Lokuarachchi and Bentulova lining up for their school photograph. I knew the teacher, Liyana; she was once my teacher too. She called out through the window, Wickramasinghe, Wickramasinghe, look what trouble we have with young people today. It had been no easy task to bring the rowdy band of girls together, she told me as they took their places inside; only after shouting out their names several times had Teacher Liyana got them to sit in order on the bench at the appointed distance from the camera where Dickwella the photographer had been patiently waiting with his assistant, Pieterson, who wore shorts and did nothing. His hair was in a bun. I have no words.

I remember it well, Teacher Liyanarachchy, I shouted back, we girls were the devils of the earth! At this, Dickwella crossed himself, disappeared under a huge black sheet that might have come from a theatre and asked the girls to smile. It's always hard to get it right, particularly when you are using such old-fashioned equipment but for the most part the picture was a success, the class lined up, uniformed, smart, global prospects.

I wish I could say the same for mine, I suddenly recalled, when I had one eye open and a boy's hand up my skirt. And I wish I could say the same for Pieterson, whose father, it turns out, has a PhD in Petro-Chemical Engineering from MIT/ROYY and is on the front cover of the next *P-CEMIT/ROYY Monthly Magazine!* I know it's wrong to make assumptions, but the truth is, Dr Pieterson's son, hair in a bun, did nothing.

Fyodor

Fyodor won a frying pan. Nothing had ever come to him for free but out-of-the-blue he received a letter informing him that he had won a frying pan in a supermarket lottery and would he be available to attend a ceremony with the mayor on such and such a date. He wondered whether it was a joke, something that either Kim or, admittedly, I, would pull. But he telephoned the number and spoke to several people all of whom were polite and a little envious; they looked forward to shaking his hand.

On the day, Fyodor wore his only suit which had a button missing and a burn mark at the knee, a small black-edged hole which might have come from a cigarette spark. He arrived on his trusty moped and we applauded as he took the stage and with it, the pan. The mayor beamed in the photo and Fyodor looked the wrong way. Lucky Fyodor, I said to him with a wink as he immediately re-mounted his bike. Fyodor isn't one for crowds so I turned my back on him to congratulate the winner of the steak-knife set.

With no particular haste, it became apparent to Fyodor that he couldn't hold the pan and steer the bike so he tried to fit it into the box on the back. The handle was, of course, too long, and hung out over the road. Obviously, this means the box's top could not be secured, only an idiot would not recognise that. I'll take it easy, Fyodor thought, swerving around a person stuck in a wheelchair in the middle of the road. We'll get you home safely, prize of my life, he said, as he turned to pat the lid of the box which immediately bounced up again.

He was negotiating the tight streets well and at a sensible pace in between fast-moving traffic all the way up to the tram lines that jutted out of the boulevard like fallen trees. Pang! Clang! over he went and out of the box flew Fyodor's prize pan, it bounced and came to a halt beneath the left front wheel of the car behind, bent into a tight isoscelean shape like an astonished mouth. I will definitely say deadpan. It also resembled a fly with wings ready for take-off. Everyone gawped as the driver dutifully reversed a little and Fyodor scraped up his lottery win.

Only a knucklehead would transport an important frying pan so riskily, shouted the driver of the car in front, who had stopped to have a look. I listened to the ceremony on the radio and was proud of you, he yelled from a standing position, I must admit to feeling something akin to love for you, don't ask me why, I own a dozen frying pans. And now to see you this way, Fyodor, the truly careless you, I feel as if I have lost a dear friend who holds with me the many secrets of closely-shared lives. I am shattered. Fyodor lowered the pan slowly and burst into tears. He really was laid out to be one of life's losers. What's more, you don't hear the word knucklehead so often these days.

Gorkzoi

The identical Gorkzoi Brothers, *The Triplets*, were closing in on me at the bus stop. I hadn't clocked them in time and it was too hot to run anywhere; as it was, many old people of the city had died of sunstroke in the previous few days; besides, I had no water on me. I'd be on the canvas in seconds. Flight impossible, fight came to the fore. But in this heat! The men – they might be clones – were wearing identical white suits with red ruffled shirts and scarlet loafers, there was sure to be a stain or two on those before the ensuing moments are out, I thought to myself as they formed a line in front of me just out of reach of a sharp kick.

I could tell Percival by his limp and he it was who decided on the triple-pillared stopping-point since it was clear from their faces they weren't going to attack me without exchanging words. Anyhow, I'd taken each of them in single combat, a doddle; and at various junctures, working strictly in pairs, I'd gone on to wallop Donovan and Milos, or Milos and Donovan, with Percival staring agape outside the book shop so I dealt him an upper-cut to shut his mouth; to crush either Milos or Donovan and Percival with bricks at work on the site; and near enough to pulverise Donovan or Milos and Percival on the church steps a fortnight ago. For good measure, I gave Percival's patella a hefty boot when he was down, as I always do, because I've had plenty of trouble with my own.

Gotcha! they exclaimed with excellent timing, hoping to surprise me. We have unfinished business, said either Donovan or Milos. Yes, said the other, we're here to finish it. But my bus will be along soon and I must see my dying aunty, and anyway it's really, really hot, I said, because I could not be sure I'd lay out all three Gorkzois before one, likely Percival, got his fists and head in on me. And to bear bruises from a Gorkzoi was laughable in my circles, I'd never live it down, they might even take my medals away. There's a transport strike, fool, said Donovan I think. You're not going anywhere said maybe Milos. So, we meet at last, said Percival, who I was meeting for the hundredth time. He winced when he switched between legs for balance. We're going to tie you to the bus stop because the people need to be heard, strikes affect their lives most egregiously, there is a massive failure of service to the wrought-upon citizens when a strike is called for a Friday and all the drivers will take a long-weekend at the beach. Percival spoke at length with some pleasing articulacy. Instead of taking you on in six-hands-to-two combat, he said, because, you're right, it is insufferably hot, we are going to make you the principal agent of resistance by tying you to the bus stop thereby expressing, almost metaphorically, how motionless we become in the service of a few days at the seaside.

It's fucking infuriating, said Milos or Donovan about nothing in particular. Cunts, said the other. But we've found you and you will satisfy our inner anger, said Percival. Externally, we see things more arty. There is Saint Sebastian in you but without the arrows. Can't we just have a smash up and be done with it, I asked, looking at my watch. Dear boy, said Percival, never swap an eye for an eye when the sun is high. He fell silent and stared at me almost quizzically, I'd no idea what he meant with his rash apothegm, he then whipped some rope from inside his jacket, his brothers following suit immediately. In a trice, they had tied them into a workable length.

I was, I must admit, fearful of being left to roast in the sun and asked if any of them had at least some water. One of the two of the three produced a flask from his white breast pocket, handed it over with a bow, and said, take your fill, we know it's hot. Then Percival piped up with *ad manus fratrum!* which I remembered from grammar school Latin and here, if you ask me, is where things got strange. Before they tied me to the bus stop, they linked arms and performed what I can only describe as a sort of ethnic dance involving two making an arch for the third to pass through while either Donovan or Milos rang bells they pulled from their pockets and Percival blew on a tin-whistle he'd had nestled behind his right ear as if it were a cigarette.

It must be said, they made a sizzling midsummer festival of three just for me. That triplets think alike was not in question as they leapt and landed with exquisite precision and synchronicity, curlicuing their way around with joy in their hearts and only the slightest of winces from Percival who was clearly, I am happy to say, in pain.

When they came to a halt, I found myself triangulated, stuck in the middle of isoscelean triplets - to think geometry was my worst subject at school - I began to drift back in time to Latin and literature, it was hot, I was reclaiming Apuleius when they re-doubled their dance around me in a triangular circle several times, upon completion fastening me tight - toe to chin - to the stop for the number 37 bus which wasn't coming anyway.

What a fine martyr you make, said Percival, smiling. As one, they took long swigs of water, and as one, the Identical Gorkzoi Brothers turned their heels on me. Good job Donovan, said, I finally deduced, Milos, throwing an arm around the grimacing triplet while Percival kept straight-legged time to their winning retreat. So, it was Donovan I'd whacked in the knee. My bad.

Bilok

On their way from the parade ground, Freimoot and Jungfleisch stopped in to see Bilok. Oh, yes, it's you, come in, said Bilok in his dressing gown. Tea? No, said Jungfleisch. We'll not stay long. That's right, said Freimoot, we've come to tell you the news, get your coat on. Why, what's up, said Bilok, sensing their urgency. Freimoot said, all right, we've cleaned up the town. We're taking you to see the criminals so you can write about them in the local news. Every scribbler loves a scoop, said Bilok, reaching for the dresser next to the front door and popping three pens into his pocket.

Bilok sat in the back of the Cortina, Freimoot in the passenger seat, Jungfleisch at the wheel. All was silent until Freimoot turned to Bilok. You like athletics, don't you, Bilok, I seem to remember a conversation a couple of years ago at the annual Party Party, am I wrong, asked Freimoot warmly. Bilok said, I watch what I can on TV. I remember a penchant for lady high-jumpers, said Jungfleisch, nose to the road ahead. Bilok reddened over and shrunk into his seat. I prefer the throwing events, he said, half-heartedly.

Get your note-pad out, said Jungfleisch as she removed her leather gloves and marched through the double doors leading to the parade ground. Bilok asked what the bundles were doing maybe seventy metres away. Freimoot said, we told you we had good news. They are the criminals, she continued, handing Bilok a pair of binoculars. What about the long poles stuck around them? Javelins, said Jungfleisch. In close-up, Bilok saw the bodies of the bundles stretched out on the grass, secured like starfish with thick twine and pegged into the ground. As the binoculars swept the distant widths of the field, Bilok saw a couple sleeping, a couple trying to free themselves and a couple with javelins sticking through them, quite dead.

What a scoop, said Bilok, scribbling away into his notebook. Yes, we thought you'd like it, here's a photograph of us. Freimoot handed Bilok a picture of the two women in athletics' vests and shorts, making a cross with their javelins. It'll be good publicity for our forthcoming election hopes, said Freimoot, it's time we dispersed the slurries of this town. Jungfleisch flew past her to launch her sporting spear with a tremendous gut roar. YEEEES, she screamed, just managing to pull up before the chalk line they'd laid down under competition rules. YEEEEES. The weapon flew miles to fall point up between the two sleeping bundles that continued to sleep. Close but no biscuit, puffed Jungfleisch. See those two trying to get away, said Freimoot to Bilok who raised the binoculars. I do, said Bilok. Here, said Freimoot, handing him a javelin.

Chicho

After dinner, we moved to Wawinmaway's round table for our usual game of cards. Once our normal tentative beginnings had given way, there was a significant increase in the stakes on the seventh-or-so hand because at least four of us, as far as I could tell slyly shifting my eyes around the table, believed we had something.

With a thousand Rambles in the middle, Gutiérrez suddenly threw both his cards facedown and leapt from his seat shouting, I'm going to leave my wife! She is in love with a woman! At this, he tore his coat from the rack and stomped out into the snow. We decided not to continue with the round and returned to one another the appropriate stakes. Get me a coconut juice would you, Chicho, said Singh to me as she collected in the cards. In doing so, she turned up Gutiérrez's pair and well if he didn't have two queens which would have been plenty to win.

Ťuganut

After a late breakfast, I found myself sitting in my favourite tree in the woods, a majestic laburnum whose golden flowery chains were budding on the branch, I bet it could tell a tale or two but trees have no memory. The August sun was high in the sky which was strange for February. There was a sound of snapping twigs on nature's carpet and who should appear beneath me but Ťuganut the chicken farmer and Oglepod the local nobleman, who removed his hunting cap and his bald pate flickered in the snooded midday light beneath the dense tendrils of the tree, my favourite tree and Oglepod owned it, some people own everything.

While from above Oglepod looked every inch the monied lord, Ťuganut looked out of breath. I heard from Vimtaz at the garage that he'd had a bit of work done on his blood pressure. He was more purple than I can ever remember him. Oglepod put a hand on his shoulder and said, we've walked a great distance now, Ťuganut, I feel your strain, I think it's time you told me about the thing that is hurting your heart. They both had fine voices and choice words. Oh, Lord Oglepod, said Ťuganut, expressing his fealty, gathering in his breath, how do you know, I feel a flush in my cheeks, is it that? Don't forget I own everything, said Oglepod with a sideways wave of his gloved left hand.

I thought it was unfair of Oglepod, a trait endemic to his ilk, to push the struggling chicken farmer in this way, but who was I twenty feet above them, sat on a thick stub of Laburnum, lost in the heavy foliage. None of which was relevant to Ťuganut. Oglepod said Ťuganut, tugging at his pockets which from up high looked empty. He then made a noise in his throat that sounded briefly like a distant hunting horn and said, things aren't happy at home, I've been sat on the settee looking at the front door for two weeks while my wife, Beulahz, has baked pies and gone to her spa and later ten-pin bowling with her joyful friends, and now there's this bridge ensemble she's frequenting. I think it's depression and I think it's both of us.

Speak on, young farmer, said Oglepod commandingly. Release the fervour. There were beads of sweat on Ťuganut's brow like tiny curtain hooks. Look, I don't feel entirely comfortable telling you my deepest secrets, Oglepod, said Ťuganut way too late, I thought you dragged me up here to talk chicken, there's also a class issue which lessens my trust. But his emotion overswayed his teeming brain and he began by looking straight up into the tree, straight at me but he must have thought I was a wood elf or something because he looked down again and continued somewhat morosely, as if scraps of his life were about to be set to a flame. I saw him gather himself into himself.

If you must know Beulahz came home last night, said Ťuganut, after her round of bridge at Reckkonsonne the Disc Jockey's, I think someone got between her and her cards and spread something nasty about me, I'll dare say it was Kalishnakaya, the hygienist, she's had it in for me since the-toilet-brush-for-Christmas Christmas. Beulahz stood against the wall next to our sashayed recess, oh how quaint, said Oglepod. Ťuganut, she said, tomorrow you're going to a therapist while I'm going out with the girls. It was never wise to question my wife. In my dreams she wears bikinis and slays dragons. At this, Oglepod raised his hand between their faces like a traffic policeman and said, that sounds like a sexual fantasy in my book and out of his Great Coat pocket he took a notepad and wrote something down with a pencil whose tip he licked before guiding it towards the page. Ťuganut turned magenta.

In short, two hours ago, he continued, I'm sat on a low minimalist couch in a room of clean lines and fractured light and the psychologist in the swivel the other side of the occasional table, his name is Znitch, how could you forget a name like that, said Ťuganut, Znitch says to me Ťuganut, Beulahz tells me you've been having a few problems at home. Perhaps you'd like to share them with me? I stared at him until I felt highly uncomfortable and said, I have nothing for you, Znitch. Very well, go out into nature and speak of what you love, Ťuganut, said Znitch, rising to open the door. And here I am, a bit out of breath, said Ťuganut, this has been in all fairness a lovely idea of yours Lord Oglepod and I'm done talking about Znitch.

And what is the thing you love, tell me what sparks your heart to make you rise from your mattress in the morning, said the lord of the manor, rubbing his hands together. Neither of them knew where this was going. Chickens, said Ťuganut. Chickens, of course! said Oglepod. Tell me about your chickens, Ťuganut, said Oglepod with haste, allow me to be your ready conduit for joy. Ťuganut's eyes lit up like laser pens, they scythed around in his purpled face. It was almost kaleidoscopic. For you a tour, said Ťuganut. You might take out your book and pencil, he said, and Oglepod complied but in his own time.

Clearly relishing his opportunity to speak about the thing he loved, Ťuganut's face began to burn but not really, as if his head was on a witches' bonfire. He took two sharp wheezy breaths and said with sudden fine clarity, from the Marianas Islands, I've a Saipan Jungle Fowl. There's an Orpington, a Marsh Daisy, a Muffed Old English Game whose cute mummy died last week, we devilled her, a Spanish Indio de León and an Empordanesa; from Turkey I've got a Sultan chicken, are you getting this down, there's a Jersey Giant, a Rhode Island Red, a Rhode Island White, there's Scots Dumpy, he lost a leg, and a Kraienköppe, whatever that is.

Oglepod's fingers were quivering like reeds in a salty breeze. Slow down a little please, my humble pencil can't keep up, he said, insincerely to my mind though I could feel his exasperation rising in plumes. Not now, said Ťuganut, not for you, not for anyone, I've not been this happy in weeks and this is what I do best. Ťuganut took another two sharp wheezy breaths, cleared his throat and said with urgent precision, I've an Ixworth, a Buckeye, an Asturian Painted Hen, a Green-legged Chicken, a Barnevelder, a Booted Bantam, a Dutch Bantam and a Japanese Bantam. After all this Ťuganut broke into a gushing sweat and began to bend at the knee, but he wasn't done, he was almost the opposite of levitating, are you getting this down, moreover, I've a Sicilian Buttercup, a Red Shaver, and a Black

Shumen; while from China, and I am coming to a conclusion, he's basically tipping over, there's the Cochin, the Nankin and the Pekin, and something called the Blue Hen of Delaware. Ťuganut's legs gave way, I think his heart had burst with all the pressure of pouring forth true love and he fell face first into the trunk below me which made shreds of the flesh around his mouth as he crumpled to the ground dead at 32. Oglepod upped sticks immediately, he tore pages out of his book, swallowed them like he did this a lot and strode briskly back to luncheon at the manor.

I laughed so hard I fell clean out of the tree and landed awkwardly on Ťuganut's corpse, something happened to my knee, but that was as nothing because I lost all feeling in my back, as I looked up through the branches at the light stroking the leaves there was no feeling and now I'm coughing up blood, disabled atop the corpse of basically a decent chicken farmer with a shredded face. I think to myself that people speak very well in these parts, with good accent and a fine choice of words, and the general level of expertise on so many things is astonishing, we certainly won't die wondering about chickens. And the August sun is high in the sky which is indeed strange for February. I wonder if Beulahz is still out with her joyful friends.

Hurst

Hurst's father, General Ritmo Stiehl, or *Mo* to absolutely nobody, telephoned me last week while I was in the supermarket. Taken aback by the preliminaries I recall bumping into several elderly shoppers and receiving some sharply-worded responses, but General Ritmo Stiehl was on the other end of my new mobile that has unbelievable features. I wondered whether for some reason he had bum-dialled me, or an *aide-de-camp* had input the number incorrectly, or the General simply mistook me, a newish friend, for someone he could talk to about the fourth son from his fifth marriage, Hurst.

The boy's gone all soft, Svenfleet, he said to me, he's just had his memoir published at the age of twenty and I do not escape scrutiny, neither do his thirty-or-so step-siblings, three sets of twins, triplets among their number and Eliot, the dwarf. Frankly the whole artsy-bloody-fartsiness of it makes me want to scream at a line of men. Yet when I called him a poet at supper last night he shouted at me, his father.

Where's the filial piety of today's generation, said the general, I have slain man and boy on the battlefield with blades that cut through steel and bone to secure the freedom he enjoys, freedom, that is, to trifle with the creative arts instead of getting on a damned horse and whipping the hide clean off it until it reaches the desired velocity. It's bringing shame on the family, all his step-brothers are in the armed services where life is easy and promotion quick.

I found myself staring at a jar of pickles. Stiehl could have been stood there staring with me, my updated audio quality is beyond comprehension. What's the matter with him for god's sakes, he said, I can hear Hurst right now in his bedroom reading something he has written aloud, is he not aware that is what mad people do? Four hundred years of yeomanry, martial conquest and inevitable death are embedded in this purple rose I am holding, he said, his voice attempting to disguise a quiver which came through loud and clear, and then an artist appears and wants to write stuff down but in his way. A historian I could understand, would encourage, supply, redeem, yield up unto, remit, promote beyond all promotions and twine to my heart as a hoop of steel, but he has no interest in that, he has made perfectly clear. He tells me, the head of the armed forces, that his pen is mightier than my sword and I am damned near pushed to prove him wrong, by god he knows how to rile his old man.

By this time I'd made it round to the bottled water aisle though I might as well have been climbing Everest because it's not every day a general asks your advice. Despite tripping up a pensioner and losing audio for a few seconds which concerned me, I went on to parry his militaristic interjections, for I knew him to be a strict man and demanding. I was polite to a fault, listened capably - as I had to our small-talk the night we met at the bar in the theatre - nothing much had caught my eye except for the 3 for 2 on Salami, I tried to empathise as best I could, I was determined to imagine what life's like to a walking bucket of high-density semen wrapped inside a total arse of a human, but I didn't get very far so I kept it in, instead merely nodding down to the pensioner on the floor.

But the time I reached the tinned cheese – excellent with the capers in aisle seven – I'd plucked up the courage to share my thoughts: thing is, General Stiehl, Sir, allow me to be blunt (my hands were shaking): Hurst is an artist. That he is the only one in your gargantuan family is, statistically, surprising. I wonder if any of your other children experience it. Yes, of course they do! he interrupted, which made me jump, The Girls! He scythed into my line of thought with a brutality bordering on murderous. I told him I was already down to 5% battery – this phone is starting to look like a waste of money – and that he shouldn't feel threatened by having a son whom he had always loved, loved among all his plentiful progeny, the teeming secrets of the General's heart had once been kept in the purse of his favourite son, Hurst, the General told me at the bar that night.

His devastation was enormously palpable and for hours after the thought itched that I was not the right friend for this. Notwithstanding, the General had listened to my words and had briefly pondered them while I blocked the way to the milk. When I take over in the coup he's first against the wall, the little bitch, he said, right when my phone went dead.

Obbladee

From my blanket in the park, I could see Obbladee with his son, Uccio. They were playing cricket. Obbladee, a life-long participant observer of the sport who had to give up because of his wonky knee, was, I thought, doing some top-quality fathering, a credit to his gender and his status. This had come about because recently Uccio had shown an interest in the game, Obbladee had told me behind the supermarket, my son had suddenly climbed up from the floor to sit next to me, ensconced as I was in a Test Match on TV, said Obbladee. Nothing televisual had otherwise interested the toddler, he added.

Uccio perched like an owl on the mismatched throw-cushions, but instead of watching the game, he watched me, in the way I said, for he was a clever little boy who realised that our reactions to what comes at us in life are far more telling than the locus of their departure or the means of their arrival. Why precisely now after seven-and-a-half years of nothing on the carpet is beyond me. He should have waited longer, he said, it was a boring 2.33 runs-an-over game between Royy South East and Royy North West, centuries' old apathetic adversaries; even the commentators had drowsed off it seemed and sure enough the facial reactions Uccio sought came packaged as serene boredom so he made his own face go just like that until dinner time.

Out there in the park, Obbladee was taking every opportunity of this quality father-and-son time that came out of nowhere like cobwebs to roll out his rusty old canon of shots, the cover drive, the sweep to leg, the dab to 3rd man, the stiff block back past the bowler. Throwing to his dad as best he could, it was also Uccio's job every time to collect the ball which means that when he came to bat after an hour or so, his face was drawn and his shoulders sagged. He had never held a cricket bat before which was obvious when his dad bowled him with a straight one first ball middle stump. Obbladee leapt into the air, screamed Howzaaaaaaat! while fist-bumping himself repeatedly and insisting Uccio hi-five him. He then took the bat straight out of his son's spotless hands and recommenced the lesson.

After thirty minutes of biffing the ball and watching his boy cover most of the park, Obbladee thought once again to give Uccio a chance, perhaps this time I'll share a secret, I'll show him how to hold the bat, he thought, as Uccio jogged drowsily towards his father, it was hot and as we know Uccio's only seven-and-a-half; he was as good as in tears, truth be told. Advice administered, Obbladee came tearing in from the end of his run-up and the ball smashed into the wickets again, triumphant Dad repeating his earlier celebration. This time though, instead of handing the bat over, Uccio whacked it into Obbladee's dodgy knee sending him down like a man drowning at sea.

When Obbladee raised his head to stretch his arms to grab his knee screamingly, Uccio raised the bat as high as he could and brought it crashing down onto his dad's brainstem, killing him instantly. Mesmerised on my blanket - it's rare out here to see more than old folk strolling around or the occasional dog frisbee – I wanted to shout something out but it was too late and I didn't want to cause unnecessary fuss. As his father's head dropped to the ground faster than a violent flashback, Uccio hurled the bat away, leapt into the air, screamed Howzaaaaaaat! while fist-bumping himself repeatedly and insisting on hi-fiving his dad's cadaver.

Six hours he sat there next to the body, the clever little lad, until his mother came with a twin on either breast to take him home. Now parricide! What a palaver. Uccio knew how to hold a bat all along. I don't know where they get it from.

Khalilford

As Thrashnappi's coffin was lowered into the cold ground, the band put together by her friends for the ceremony, none of whom could play an instrument, struck up 'Time's up, see you soon, safe journey home!' It had been a hit in Royy's ale houses for a number of years. A Geoffreydots! remix went global. It was an odd final request. They didn't butcher it because there was nothing to butcher. We only knew what tune it was because Selseme told us. Aarel broke his violin bow, Selseme's squeezebox fell apart and Helpchet dropped the mic long before it should have been permissible. Unimpressed, we few stood around, our black lapels snapping up in the drizzly wind, not knowing where to look so we looked down which was pertinent. It was a funeral and everything was mismatched. Khalilford the priest was on his last legs. He's next.

The unfortunate Thrashnappi had been knocked down stone dead by her boyfriend Lievchop who'd whipped into her drive on his motorbike as she rushed out to greet him and had inadvertently battered her with a vast wild yam he'd brought for supper. The town was in shock. Everyone had estimated a better death for her. Her last words were to mumble the ale house hit. Lievchop was devastated, he'd almost been at the point of loving her, the new sensation in his chest told him so. He's barely spoken to anyone since, and then only to ask for money. He hadn't joined the mourners graveside, he was sitting on his fateful bike leaning into a blooming magnolia. The garage manager had felt deeply Lievchop's loss and agreed to change the oil for half price. Lievchop left them a dodgy cheque. Graveside, Khalilford the priest was making righteous signs with his hands and intoning the appropriate devotion, he'd done this a thousand times, I've got them in my palm, he thought to himself and he lifted his eyes towards the sky and said 'Rise from here to your new throne, Thrashnappi', which was all too much for her brother Baz who jumped into the grave and tore the lid from her coffin. We were astonished, we were many things really, we'd all taken the afternoon off, we were getting wet in the persistent drizzle, half of us were crying, some for the dead girl.

The sight weighed heavily on Khalilford who slumped to one knee. Thrashnappi's mother went to him, lay a hand on his shoulder, and did beam down upon him, at which he rose in splendid rejuvenation. The other pocket of guests stared at each other, no-one quite knowing what to do with this sudden once-in-a-lifetime interjection. There was a young man tearing into his sister's coffin trying to pull out her shroud. Stop that, someone thought to say. Our restraint was saintly. Standing on his saddle for a better view, Lievchop could take it no longer. He zipped up his leather jacket, jumped down and in a trice barged through the modest gathering and was in the dirt next to Baz, they had an arm each. I cared for her deeply, said Baz, tugging hard, well it was me she ran out to, said Lievchop, this should tell you everything. He jerked Thrashnappi's left arm around until it loosened. You see, I cared for her deeply too, he said.

Amid the consternation and concern six feet up, there were precious few instruments left but Keegan managed to let out a trumpet blast, Old Gedge farted at length and Khalilford was heard to say 'Never in all my years' – which are themselves coming to a conclusion, someone said quick as a flash but too loud. A couple in our small gathering of black-clad mourners shouted at the boys to get out, good luck with that I thought. What transgression is this! we bellowed in the heaving rain. Those whom the gods wish to destroy they first make mad.

It should be obvious by now that Thrashnappi's arms came off. It was always heading that way. Stood waving one each in death's quagmire, the bandages split, the rotten flesh peeling away, bones on show, Baz caught a good one to the face while Lievchop took a dead hand clean to the genitals. I will say I loved her then, said Baz, ducking a blow. I will say I loved her more than you, said Lievchop, all the while swiping at Baz's legs. They were masked by wet mud, seething with resentment, eyeballing one another furiously and swatting away with Thrashnappi's arms. The rain intensified and I started to think what a great landscape painting this would make when Thrashnappi's uncle, Galvin, put his hand in mine, our fingers entwined, it felt like I was pulling at strands of tobacco, I succumbed.

Only when Thrashnappi's corpse was a series of putrefying swatches in puddles of crud did exhaustion get the better of the boys and they climbed out. Waiting white vans took them away. They are broken and will not be easily fixed. We were left to discuss precisely how we should bury Thrashnappi, there were bits everywhere, her grave was a swamp, there were still tears though it was allergy season, someone reminded us, as if we could be more drenched. Raymund suggested erecting a waterproof awning over the scene so that Thrashnappi's remains may be gathered with dignity while Wichtler wanted to fill it in and pat it down immediately.

There are funerals every day in town and this sort of thing happens more than you might think. I get to as many as I can. It is almost as if we can't communicate well with the living and only in the midst of death do our deepest emotions break through the surface. Royy is not an easy continent. They say we live meaningless existences, we are impulsive, then we tell them to get lost and something breaks out. One thing's for sure, a lifetime round here has done for Khalilford.

Muharry

From our vantage point, we assumed the argument had not concluded well. Shariff had thrown his shoe at Berryman, which hit her in the neck. Enraged, Berryman threw her shoe back which caught Shariff flush on the forehead. Seething, Sharif al-Aswad threw his other shoe back but instead of hitting Berryman he hit Tamayaki, the greengrocer, bang on his balding pate.

Tamayaki was wearing rubber galoshes. Off came the first, hitting al-Aswad in the chest which made him barrel backwards like something indescribable. The second galosh Tamayaki threw was a disaster. Passing on horseback was Samira Xax, the beautiful daughter of the loathed local ruler, Maksimovich. It bounced off the hind of her gelding, A Thousand Islands, who whinnied and reared.

A skilled horsewoman, Xax soon restored equine calm. She was in full regalia, leather waders up to her waist. She daintily dismounted, removed the right wader in such a way as to engage the attention of the men of the town, and threw it at Tamayaki, striking him in the heart and killing him instantly. Pandemonium ensued.

Maksimovich was not far behind his daughter in his carriage and on arrival ordered the execution of everybody in sight and out of it. Further pandemonium ensued until a group marched over to Bill, the Bootmaker. They returned satisfied and laden to see an angry crowd with historic complaints surrounding Maksimovich and then doing something that made his head come off. A horrified Xax quickly remounted, one wader absented, but no matter. Bill the Bootmaker had run up a boot so large and of such thick leather, it took twenty men to carry it, it easily fit over Maksimovich's head and his daughter and A Thousand Islands and the carriage A Thousand Islands was still attached to before they nailed it for good to the ground in the middle of the town square. Maksimovich's body they left for vultures, so hated was he.

And do you not know, Muharry, said my companion, Bill's boot will now become a shrine for bootmakers the world over? Thousands will visit each month, dedicating piles and piles of single boots for good luck to the skull, skeletons – human and equine – and whatever is left of the carriage.

As a mother and law abiding-citizen, I could only reply, how, of all places, could such a thing possibly happen here?

O'Grymyth

Seamus O'Connell, BB Shawl's boyfriend, was in mortal danger. I'd watched the young lovers playing on the steep banks of a swollen, rushing river one autumn evening, daring one another to get closer to the water's edge. But Seamus had slipped and was now clinging for life to an old iron chain-link that boats were probably once tied to. He might be swept away any moment. BB Shawl was screaming down to him and Seamus was screaming back but as far as she dared lower herself from the top of the bank down, she couldn't stretch to reach the grasping hand of her man. Then she saw me and cried, for the love of God, Balthazar O'Grymyth, do something!

But I remember when Seamus O'Connell and BB Shawl skipped the water safety video in 5th form PSHE and went to the shopping centre instead. Otherwise, she would have known that the thing to do is take your trousers off and each grab a leg end, thereby doubling the length available. Poor Seamus's grasp finally gave and he went under the torrid tide from which he emerged three weeks later. His putrefying body was spotted by his sister, Tally, as she rode her bike along the bank one evening and it made her a non-believer her entire life, which was to be short.

Demarbleharden

Demarbleharden won a reality TV contest whose spangling prize was a ready-built two-story house with three rooms modest in size and square in shape. From my hot air balloon, I could see two adjoining squares with the third centred on top of them although a walk-round the outer perimeter would also give the basic setting.

Homeless before the show but wowing millions with his unwashed Troubadour tear-jerkers and sleeping in the park, Demarbleharden immediately prepared to embrace his new-found fame and domestic fortune. Personally, I consider him mediocre. There being no garden to tend to – the house was some way from the town's leafy suburbs – he fashioned a kitchen, a bedroom, and a writing studio in which he might entertain guests or fans, this being the room upstairs that partly spanned the other two.

The kitchen walls were white, the bedroom red and the studio given a soft-tinged green. All fittings were included, the bed was huge, the fridge fit for a very fat king and the plush *chaise-longue* and amity seats perfectly comfortable, particularly for those who'll have to take two buses to get here, thought Demarbleharden as he put up the bunting on the front door. No-one told him once off screen all interest died.

He didn't have connectivity because the tall iron electricity pylons that surrounded the house at mid-distance ensured all signals were scrambled at best. He was not to know that nobody would come to use the amity chairs and that he'd have to drive a mile to the nearest store for food and even further for computer items and he didn't have a licence or a car.

The truth is another reality contest had started and people preferred to stay at home to watch the latest fiercely fought battle between a ventriloquist, a plate spinner and a woman with her acrobatic dog. Since the plate spinner was a homeless waiter, the massive audiences – even young children stayed up late – threw as one its affection at him and he was sure to win, despite the fact the dog could do a summersault, though he had to live with his owner in a car. The ventriloquist's puppet's head dropped off, effectively terminating his participation. There were whispers but I am not a gossip.

Tragically for Demarbleharden, he had fallen from favour, before favour spitefully whipped open her coat to reveal a negligee and perfect beach body, and all coming off the sweaty back of a rival show hot on his heels. He had felt like a million dollars and – fair enough – had been blessed with liveable digs for his talent.

His eventual disappointment turned to drug dependency and some sickness of the mind. He waited day after day at the front door, the bunting wilting, for fans to come and photograph him moving around doing things before he noticed no birds were singing between the pylons and nothing grew. Thus an island, how could Demarbleharden have known his only nod to fame would be a three square-roomed apartment quite off the tourist route? Anyway, the red bedroom was a ridiculous idea, it seems fitting that I sleep in it alone, and the soft-tinged green recalls my marijuana days, he thought one rueful night.

Neither did he know the latest prize was for four rooms blocked together right next to his, inside the pylons, chances are he'll be neighbours with a plate spinner. They have already commissioned several more series.

Rapsomanikis

Down on the beach, Dev, Kefalas, and Kwang'o were having a vigorous discussion so I bad them good-day. Hello, there, Rapsomanikis, said Dev. You're looking thinner than when I last saw you. Are you over-exercising, asked Kwang'o. I swerved the issue by telling them that their conversation struck me as so vivid I had to come and see what it was about. Oh that, said Dev.

There's three of us, one boat, see the island over there, four oars, one life jacket, 5% left on the only walkie-talkie. The challenge is to get each of us to the island and back on the boat individually and in pairs but without ever being with the same person twice. Not saying a word, I walked off, because this reminded me of a puzzle with animals and a vegetable that I struggled with at school and I'll never forget that day years ago with Kefalas laughing at me all the way home.

Terrance

Krakoff was playing with the python he'd had since it was a little squiggle, now become a 2-metre-long death machine which was curling its way around its owners neck, which Krakoff loved, he often focussed on its qualities, the skin, the humid, briny scales, like a sticky scarf. Pythons are the current pets of choice. You can't move round here for pythons, they're very loyal apparently. But this afternoon, Krakoff's playful snake tightened like never before, it felt more like a rubbery spasm to Krakoff who tried to peel his pet away but just as the serpent found an extra bit of strength so, it seems, Krakoff failed to find his, the python was around his neck and shoulders and things have shifted from light-hearted to emergency and suddenly Krakoff is thinking, fuck, this is it, I've met my murderer, his name's Terrance.

Krakoff ran straight for the front door and was in the street in seconds, with a six-foot snake flailing round his shirt collar. He dropped to his knees at the curb. A saloon car of the continental type slowed down and Krakoff saw a look of general horror and a girl in the back - nine maybe ten – taking pictures on her phone. A second car pulled up – a retro two-door – Krakoff was on his back by this time, Terrance was constricting his life away, he really hadn't planned on checking out like this, things went a bit blurry for him but definitely a thick-set woman got out of the second car and took a pair of industrial wire cutters from her extensive trunk. She put a foot down on the snake's upper body and with a muscular embrace of the tool clipped Terrance's head clean off. The beast writhed and soon fell still as a lopped branch.

When the driver of the retro two-door saw the girl's phone she went over, stuck her hand in the window, grabbed it, stomped on it, it was in pieces on the dusty pavement, the girl couldn't cry because her whole face had closed down. Krakoff's saviour picked up the snake's head, chucked it and the cutters back in the trunk, got back in her retro two-door and drove away. The continental saloon did a U-turn and went off in the other direction, the girl had been reunited with her lungs and was screaming. Krakoff was left to regain full consciousness and in the rain that fell fleetingly on him remove Terrance's dead heft. It was a Friday and several other Fridays have also yielded similar encounters. Krakoff had a nasty bruise around his neck but then so have many others and that's fashion for you.

Lourença

We hadn't seen Sanders for months and suddenly there he was behind the window of a restaurant alone at a table for two. What an extraordinary sight. We poured through the door. A ladies' man if ever there was one, Sanders had aged about 1000 years and had hair growing out of his ears which drooped down to the pockets on his ragged cardigan.

Sanders looked up and said, this chickpea soup's disgusting, and we all laughed at him and said, Sanders, Sanders, what have you become? Shave your ears for mercy's sake! You'll have to shout louder, Sanders said, I can't hear you, it's all fuzz. We repeated what we said like carol singers at full blast. Don't you tell me how to wear my hair, particularly you, Patrícia Lourença, replied an irate Sanders, pointing a clump at me, which was odd because I'm someone else. He responded by dipping the tips of his ear hair into the soup and sucking them thoroughly into his once handsome mouth. What a falling off there had been.

But not of hair. It happened that a passing waiter spotted Sanders' behaviour and said, hey you have to use the spoon we provide. It's one thing letting you in here with your alien coiffure but this latest lack of hygiene is unacceptable. Defiantly, Sanders strained another twine the same way. I felt it was increasingly sexual. And a third time, a reckless challenge to authority surely. We shouted, Sanders, Sanders, leave with us now so we can help you restore your ears to something more bearable.

As Sanders slid a skewer of hair from his mouth like a furred dagger taken from the sheath, the waiter hit him over the head with his sandwich tray and disappeared into the kitchen. We were speechless. Next, the manager arrived to see Sanders delicately jagging his clump with the tip of his tongue and hit him in the face with the empty chair opposite before ambling back into the kitchen.

Sanders bounced backwards with violence and recoiled face down in his soup. He made a mess while we made an odd choir, mouths frozen into gaping circles. Sanders of course couldn't hear a thing. It was one of the stranger evenings we have known. On the way home we surreptitiously glimpsed passers-by for ear hair and there was a slew of it on every auricle. Sanders' admirers are rising.

Mutone

I was strolling in the early spring sunshine when Kumar and Storno jogged towards me on the path to the cafeteria. It had been an age since we last met and I had heard through a friend of a friend they'd fallen on hard times. It made me glad to see them indulging in physical activity, it lessens depression I had recently read online. We waved to each other from a short distance and when they arrived at my shoulders, they stopped, both panting a little, and sweating, one either side. I gave them my biggest smile though forewent the usual offer of a hug.

You two look happy, I said. Ah, Mutone, it has been a while, replied Kumar. Since we last met back at the CEO's Annual Ball, we have been through difficult times, but things changed for us about a year ago when an unexpected employment opportunity arose for two able-bodied women. We found work as diggers on the metropolis' inaugural underground station. It's been a life-saver for me, said Kumar, food on the table. Me too, and we're having another baby, said Storno, patting her stomach. Is it dangerous, I asked? Not particularly, said Storno. They gave us a spade each and showed us where they'd like the hole to start and left us to it. We've been at it for nearly ten months now, said Kumar, showing me her calloused hands. But they do pay on time, said Storno. You must be some way down by now, I said out of curiosity. Better than that even, Mutone, we have dug out escalators, ticket office, elevators, electronic signage, tracks have been laid from one end of the platform to the other, advertising space has been carved into existence, and a self-service sandwich machine installed next to the emergency exit. They are very happy with our work, they told us. And all the while, after our work is done and we return to the daylight, we have been jogging together, above ground as it were, moving horizontally, maintaining a balance if you like.

I'm not surprised they like your work, I replied, incredulously. Quite simply, I am flabbergasted by the power of human achievement you two have shown. But I do have one question for you before you get on with your jog. With only one underground station, where's anybody going to go? With that they both shrugged. Storno said, we hadn't thought of that and Kumar added, that brain of yours is probably why you never fell on hard times, Mutone, and off they went, tipping their strong legs into a run. I wished them and their men and children well from a growing distance and was left to ponder whether it is not indeed dangerous to dig out electronic signage with a spade just because Kumar and Storno said it wasn't.

Benkenkopf

Once a year the great inventors of Royy converge to the east for the Innovation Day Festival which in fact lasts three days. A committee was set up to rename it but nothing got done. The lawn of Fine Fescue grass set aside on Ypressent farm was immaculate, the trillion blades cut to size and soft underfoot reminded me of the recent recruitment campaign by the armed services. A dominant oak tree was the centrepiece, while lines of bluebells ordered the separate areas for the continent's wackiest boffins who had brought their fill of futurity across harsh terrain in order to make a few Shockles on the side. And who knows, one day an inventor might win the Innovation Day Festival Prize of a golden question mark the size of a Heckler sausage, mongered by Smelsette several years ago and never awarded due to the general uselessness of the inventions.

Ypressent, the perennial judge, was criss-crossing the bluebells trying to work out precisely what all this shit actually was. She was followed by a small crowd of people who didn't know either but wanted to stare at stuff. Shaded to the left of the oak, Al-sham was busy exhibiting his latest attempt at wooden bathing suits while Uhwhal had set up his piano for the bed-ridden. Around the trunk Mills was presenting his edible paint to no-one while Bèréniè was to the right, demonstrating her dogbrella on a cat because no dogs had been allowed on the farm since Ypressent's beloved German Shepherd, Stikki, drowned in the irrigation debacle. Ask me, Ypressent got away with one there. From high in the sky our scene might present shifting characters on a novelty barometer. Unusually, Benkenkopf was nowhere to be seen but then again he'd turned up last year with his liquid slippers and came last. He sold one and went bankrupt. His shame was immense. The cat rolled from under the brolly several times, much to the frustration of Bèrénië who was working the watering can hard. It sidled away to kill a snail at which point Bèrénië was all dogbrella and no cat.

This went on for 72 hours. It's only once a year but it's an age when you're involved. It's not something I look forward to. There is a festival atmosphere but downbeat. There is a food tent but I bring my own. There is alcohol but I recently abjured. There is invention but no-one knows why. In the shade of the mighty oak a table was set up with Smelsette's golden question mark on a plinth. Ypressent was swapping between various clipboards, asking questions like won't they go rotten in the water and what if it falls on the sick person and what possible use could that have and have you lost your cat again? It was dawn and dusk and dawn and dusk and deadlock. The people began to get restless while continuing to stare, a strange disjunction.

On the third morning as the sun was sliding slowly between ten-to and five-to, a net untucked and fell from the branches of the tree to snare to perfection the competitors who made an assortment of sounds as they were hoisted high into the air by a hand-powered winch that poked out of the oak's foliage. The weight-to-energy ratio was through the roof everyone was agreeing when a gloved hand peeked mischievously through the deeply-indented leaves.

This will transform the fishing industry, said someone who'd been paying attention. Not to mention washing the dishes, said someone who hadn't. The restless net was hanging high in the branches when who should follow the hand out of them and onto a sturdy timber limb but Benkenkopf. My humiliation is concluded, he said, looking down over the people. Let us out, shouted the boffins but there wasn't much energy for it, this had gone on long enough. Benkenkopf leapt from the tree to land perfectly on the ground. He once showed me some Special Services photos from when he was a younger man. They were horrifying. There was warm applause. Ypressent handed Smelsette's golden question mark to Benkenkopf who lifted it high above his head to further warm applause, the question soundly answered. He was elated and vengeful, which looked amazing on his face.

Don't forget us, shouted the inventors through the rough hessian strands. They resembled a choir of angry, ragged angels. These people are fucking crazy. There are four quacks in white coats suspended high above the ground in a net. It's not exactly new, said one of the women who'd been looking up, but its economy leaves me breathless. There was a hum among the crowd. Soon enough Benkenkopf had taken several orders and everyone packed up until next year. There was an oil slick where the food tent had been and a small but dissipating buzz about what had gone down, or, indeed, up.

The oak tree looks magnificent from a distance, its craggy heft centres Ypressent's lawn which will recover. The net gives the foliage a trippy vibe, swirls and colours. Inside, looking very glum, are four of Royy's great inventors. I don't know why I said great, nobody's coming for them, this we agreed as soon as our backs were turned. Benkenkopf did fine out of it but you'd have to say the world of innovation is going to take a hit. Invent your way out of that, you four! You lot must eat one another or die, I said giving them a wave, winding up the window, and easing off into the distance. Actually make that eat one another *and* die!

Matei

The village women had gathered in a circle around the War Memorial and were engaged in rigorous debate. I heard them from my window and went out to investigate. The sun was roasting. I asked one of the women courteously whether she minded if I listened in and she nodded to me, saying, you're Matei, aren't you? You're a good sort and are as welcome here as anyone, particularly as a man, we don't discriminate she said, gesturing me onto a throw-cushion.

Looking around, the heat of the debate was taking place between Tskitishvili, Stoika and Winifred, with occasional intelligent insertions by Mungyung and Dillinger. After much to-ing and fro-ing, Tskitishvili declared aloud, I will not have my husband go to another war. He needs his time in the clinic like the rest of them, we're all without our men because our men went to war, those who aren't dead are recovering in the clinic, she concluded, somewhat repetitively. I work part-time in the clinic, said Mungyung. I didn't know that, replied Winifred. We've shed our tears, said Stoika, now is the time for peace. But what if the enemy invades, asked Winifred. Yes, interesting point, interjected Dillinger, our men might have to go to war by way of defence. I'd rather myself go to war than my husband again, said Stoika. At this there was a gentle ripple out into the crowd of women which turned into a flurry of small groupings, nods, ideas discussed, general assent and the emergence of an energetic consensus.

It turned out Mungyung wasn't so occasional at all. She was best friends with a military supplier whom she telephoned immediately. From her, Mungyung ordered 250 uniforms, berets, sub-machine guns, grenades, bullet-proof bras, pistols, daggers, ground-to-air missiles, night-goggles, a dozen of the latest American tanks and brooches with tiny roses encrusted in ruby. She got free postage and next-day delivery which came late morning in a rolling convoy.

By early evening, everything was set. Tskitishvili would give the command to Stoika, who would in turn give the command to Winifred but exclude Mungyung and Dillinger. Winifred would then give the signal for the women to dress for war, in order to show the hardware at their disposal and the alacrity with which it is possible to arm oneself to the teeth. They stood lined, brilliantly drilled, Stoika performed a walk-by and only had to adjust one brooch. They were ready. By radio, Winifred sent the message for the men to be brought from the clinic to the War Memorial and now. The time had come to rehearse defensive attack.

Ryöyksenæ

Ryöyksenæ owned a moped, a *Kikausha-nywele* he called it (in the local language, *Hairdryer*, which is hard to say, so when I'm talking I'll call it a little bike instead). Ryöyksenæ owned a little bike. The two-wheeler was perfect for the city's clogged arteries and with considerable weaving got him wherever he needed on time. In its dotage, largely unloved by its owner, the little bike chugged on like an exhausted horse pulling a carriage full of tourists. Rarely did Ryöyksenæ throw money at it which explains to me the little bike's bruised exterior.

I can plan my busy schedule between jobs with my old *Kikausha-nywele*, Ryöyksenæ poured forth some months ago when we met at the darts club. I haven't assigned it a gender or come to any decision regarding a name, but that said, said Ryöyksenæ, sexless and devoid of identity beyond its obvious *Kikausha-nywele*-ness, it's never let me down zigzagging crosstown, probably twenty Kfaffs a week to run which over the course of a year still isn't very much for a man with three jobs, though it might well be too much for lower-income colleagues and I am sorry, he said.

I'm getting off track and soon you'll understand why. Ryöyksenæ shared the following news with me only today on the packed number 63 bus, which was dragging its sorry way into town. We were pilchards out of the tin and into the sizzling pan. Not being one for small talk, Ryöyksenæ said, there you are, Hartful, it must have been three months and you're still struggling to get your darts in the bullseye, I hear, you look tired, have you had bad news? His eyes worked slowly across my forehead; it felt almost angelic. Why are you on a bus? I asked him. *Kikausha-nywele*, he replied, a look of sad mischief sweeping across his face, it was quite a sight. Ready, he asked?

I was ready all right. The 63 was rickety across our ancient capital's rugged cobblestones, sworn enemy of shock absorbers, nightmare for bikers. I remember one ending up under a bus in the rain. His body seemed strange to me, it was broken in several directions. Ryöyksenæ would have to speak over many heads which darted as water droplets fell, the bus itself was sweating. Ryöyksenæ is also eighteen inches taller than me and it was hard to get perspective, crammed as I was, among sodden midriffs.

I know Ryöyksenæ to be a witty man even though his face had changed, I think, with time and for the darker. Perhaps something was coming that would pit his humour against his anger, I thought, without knowing a thing really, but I was excited at the prospect of what might turn out to be completely nothing; that maybe His Tallness had just caught the sun or something. Someone's crotch was under my chin.

This weekend, commenced Ryöyksenæ, no change in the unbearable weather, people were sinking into pavements, I park up my *Kikausha-nywele*, pick up my boy, and we go to mine, across the city, on the bus together. 48 hours later, we've done a bit of parkour, my knee's not right, same return journey. He's back upstairs with his mum, I'm kerbside. I put the key in the lock, the *Kikausha-nywele* collapses into two perfect halves. My tall friend, up to whom I look in every way, swished his hand down like an executioner her sword. Longways, he said, tires, stand, handlebar, dashboard, foot platform, saddle and box on the back, all filleted. They fell in opposite directions onto open tarmac. Like a devilled chicken.

You're gawping, said Ryöyksenæ, which was embarrassing for me. Someone, continued my tall friend, has taken a chainsaw to my *Kikausha-nywele* in the middle of a crowded suburb; a surgical gutting. They left it perched just so, said Ryöyksenæ. He made a box shape with his hands, it felt fallacious. It took only the slightest nudge to watch aghast as both halves fell to the ground in almost poetic motion, bounce a bit, he said, kick up some dust before coming to a beautifully symmetrical slaughterhouse halt. I had to leap back briskly. Crowds gathered instantly and at unbidden respectful distance; this was performance art of the highest calibre.

What loathsome individual could have done such a heinous thing, I asked? A genius, replied Ryöyksenæ, as the bus screeched and we all lurched forward into each other's paunches. I was impressed how Ryöyksenæ kept on his feet given this was not his transportation of choice. A genius, he repeated, as we all lurched back into place again as if pushed by a mighty palm. This was no fly-by-night kid who'd just had the mother of all rows with his father, oh, no. Whoever performed this operation was highly trained, probably a degree at a creative institution or coming from a line of chainsaw artists. I understand, I said. But why your bike among all? It was the oldest there, he said, there's no beauty left to destroy, which in itself is beautiful is it not, he said, quizzically.

The *Kikausha-nywele* was a nobody-in-waiting. You know what thrills me most, he asked, as we shuffled to and fro. That the artist, the genius, this person of vision, so innovative, such a wanker, will never dare show a face because the locals might have a thing or two to say to them about this type of behaviour. But then again the locals are not the type to be too bothered.

Get this, Ryöyksenæ said, putting an arm down onto my shoulder and squeezing. The nefarious butchery was seized upon by The Culture Ministry as an important work of local art, contemporary, cutting-edge, they said, without a trace of irony. It was sealed off that evening, placed under a huge glass case covered by an interior curtain which slides back when a one Kfaff coin is placed in the slot, about 60 seconds in the opening and closing to take in what is quite possibly the greatest piece of conceptual art pushed through this country's birth canal for centuries.

Copy-cats have since started up across the city but none has the precision of the mighty Bifurcator of my *Kikausha-nywele*, said Ryöyksenæ. The crowds are endless, security barriers have been put in place – and this on a tight street in a twisty part of town – Kfaffs are pouring in, the iconic bike hailed as a future winner of something for conceptual art with metal involved. I'm on 10%, I cut a deal with the mayor's chief-of-staff. I'll not make any attempt to move it for the course of its cultural iconicity which at this point in time seems eternal.

The bus groaned to a final halt and we alighted at the terminus. As I was re-arranging myself, Ryöyksenæ asked, what if they'd chosen to cut it the other way, separating back from front, a handlebar-less saddle, a saddle-less set of handlebars, more Tom & Jerry, don't you think, far less sincere, got lucky there, didn't I? But you could still use the box, in fact you'd have two boxes now, I cried out, as Ryöyksenæ hiked up his untailored trousers, stepped down, wiped his brow and disappeared into another crowd.

Chchton

My friend Gelsey Lamentahalb loves her job, she's a nurse in the mental hospital where all the local head-cases end up. Once a week she comes round after work and we drink schnapps and eat bagels while she fills me in on all the loony goss. Chchton, she began yesterday as we sat next to the rude ambience of my television set, have I got a tale from the funny farm for you! Let's hear it, let's hear it, Gelsey Lamentahalb, I said excitedly as I scrunched my toes up my trainers like an unopened jar of pickles, uncomfortably so because for some time I've thought that Gelsey has a contaminated imagination.

Well, Gelsey began, having made very firm eye contact, either the King of Bomania has been admitted to Room 12 or it's some sicko who reckons himself a bit; it's a cosy number, *en suite*. But surely you can tell straight away, I said, you're professionals, you'll not be fooled so easily. Here's the thing, Chchton, said Gelsey, removing her third bagel from the silver tray, he was dropped off in a Bentley with 10,000 Zlang and a nifty crown in his backpack. He was apparently intending to blow up forty-two million people, so we thought we'd keep him in. Somehow, I still can't imagine a king with a backpack, I thought quietly to myself. He's also very well spoken, he has a delicacy of language I thought I'd never experience, said Gelsey, brushing something slowly off her thigh.

Chchton, for the first time in my career, she said, I find myself fascinated by a lunatic. His name is Randolph and yesterday morning he abandoned the Kingdom of Bomania over which his family have ruled quite monstrously for 500 years. He even began his journey on muleback. We are warrior stock, he said, fearless, fighting is our favourite thing whereas our womenfolk bake pies. Sadly, King Randolph's attempts to emote with his body were chastened by the straight-jacket. He could only shuffle his arms around like puppies in a blanket. He told me I had exceptional eyes. He sang several folk songs to me after I'd made him drink from the little cup. I was surprised by the quality of the acoustics even though Room 12 is the best we have.

I say, Gelsey, this sounds like dangerous territory for a mental health provider such as yourself. But Chchton, she said, how often do men of such obvious breeding and genetic superiority end up in a psychiatric ward? I was surprised she didn't know and I was just about to answer when she burst into tears and said, I've fallen in love with a mad monarch in exile! At this, Gelsey stood up and I saw lots of little crumbs drop from her skirt to the ground. I'm on duty first thing, said Gelsey, wiping her eyes, licking the tips of her fingers and moving to the heavy-set front door. He's going to write me a poem, Gelsey sighed and said, he's every inch a king for me.

I listened to the gravel crunch under the wheels of her coupe car and waved her away to her bed and her dreams. She'd likely have a busy morning. She made no proper mention of King Randolph possibly faking it which I find extraordinary because Gelsey Lamentahalb is an experienced psychiatric nurse, a woman of some passion bundled up with a fair-to-middling intellect, and she's crushing on some aristo-doozy who's rocked up demanding attention. It's not often the goss is as classy at that. She is perhaps wilfully ignoring the overarching tenet of her career in that the staff where she works are also completely crazy, are complete mirror images. But then they do often say these days the lunatics have taken over Royy's many asylums. I for one was so swept up in the whole thing, I clean forgot to tell Gelsey that the King of Bomania was on the foreign news last night, declaring war on the neighbouring Republic of Glis and no-one noticed the plastic tag on his wrist.

Otowongu

Immediately after the evening's event an older lady with eyeglasses on a looping gold chain approached me to ask if I would sign her copy of my poem that I had read in considered tones to a well-turned-out audience twenty minutes previously. I felt embarrassed and looked around in the hope that none of the other readers was watching. Coast clear, I agreed and she pulled a smart, gold pen from her bag.

I enjoyed listening to you and will treasure the memory of your reading as I sit by the fire with your autographed work in this wonderful magazine, she said. The little finger of her left hand was inserted at page thirty-five which suddenly fluttered into life beneath my chin. Under your name, she said, handing me the weighty pen, sign there, such a beautiful poem, Deryck.

I blinked hard. But my name is John, I replied, not Deryck, you have the wrong reader. I remained of good cheer while repeating the misunderstanding a little louder. No, she said, unruffled in her persistence, you are Deryck, Deryck Harris. No, I am John, John Otowongu, I replied, and my poem is on page forty-seven. Still no sign of anything whatsoever amiss, she looked around the bookstore and asked, which one is Deryck? Though he was only two readers before me I had no way of remembering and sent her off to the opposite corner to meet her next mistake.

The older lady with eyeglasses on a looping gold chain returned almost immediately. She waved the magazine open to show me Deryck Harris' signature in glistening biro above my name at the foot of my poem on page forty-seven, the one I had read out around thirty minutes ago. Deryck Harris signed, she said, unforgivably brusque for my liking, notwithstanding her age, pushing the magazine back into my hands.

For amusement, I turned to the poem on page thirty-five to

return the compliment but I saw Deryck Harris' signature repeated, this time above his own name and work.

And now, she said, offering her open palms, I'll take my magazine home and treasure the memory.

Newlyses

Five minutes before my VIP tour was due to begin I turned left at the M.I.S.C. sign on the highway and into the vast car park of the new Military-Industrial-Shopping-Complex, the exterior of which, from a distance, looks like a giant rhino horn stood on its end. I parked my comfortable cruiser and clipped across the crowded car park sensing an opportunity to get to know another side of this great continent of ours. A call came from the ministry when I was playing table tennis with Lockey in the basement. Lockey said it ruined his concentration but actually he's just not that good. I should be here at this and this time, said the voice, I'll be shown round by top brass and asked to share the experience with worthy parties back home. I think they thought I was someone else. Notwithstanding the defence forces' glaring clerical error – surely a sign of slackening standards – it felt like a potential in, so I ran it past my husband, had a whip-round in town and got myself a briefcase full of cash.

I was ushered through the impressive double doors and into the grand air-conditioned lobby by a dour army type, General Newlyses, and a junior aide, Afterblie. They escorted me to level nineteen where escalators were zigzagging across shop signs and gun-toting bikinied men and women were barging through rowdy queues outside make-shift boutiques that sell shares in the enemy's oil. In every store, Newlyses pored over Smartboard maps that patriots of our great continent were busy re-drawing. His entire life's work has been shopping, his name badge was not straight, and his medals jangled awkwardly. Afterblie had tufts of hair in her ears.

We dropped into a boisterous seminar on *Land-Grabs and the Unmanned Drone* which was rammed to the rafters with every colour and creed Royy has to offer. I sat next to a group of ne'er-do-wells who were selling an army by electronic mail. I kept a side eye on my briefcase throughout. As we carefully re-negotiated, or barged through, the shoppers outside, General Newlyses announced with a wave of his heavily-embroidered sleeve that because global domination is a hot ticket, sometimes buyers get pushy at M.I.S.C., yet the robust commercial atmosphere is well-intentioned and on target towards fostering respectful communication between our great continent and her sworn domestic and international foes. Afterblie hadn't said a word. She must have felt me looking at her because she put a finger to her lips in the silent sign and shrugged.

Surveying as much as is humanly possible, Newlyses stood on the tips of his toes and spread his arms out in a delicate circle which he clasped shut with his fingertips and slowly lowered himself to his normal stance almost callisthenically. I felt like I'd witnessed the gesture of a minor deity, remarkable for a military man, it was a moment of pure Morse-code for the body, I believe. This is for you, Effov, said the general, handing me a coupon for a happy massage on the house, level sixty-nine, I wasn't impressed. And what's more, he said stridently in the manner of an owner, everything and everyone in the Military-Industrial-Shopping-Complex is for sale. I looked at Afterblie, she looked at Newlyses, Newlyses nodded, Afterblie looked at me, opened her mouth and said, I'm in the silent corps, that's all I can say. Newlyses nodded again impassively when I thought empathy might have been the card to play. It couldn't be easy for her. I hope she finds opportunities to compensate for her dire existence.

I took a moment to peer over the safety rail but lost count of women and men everywhere selling tanks and jets and bombs and night goggles that do look cool and uniforms and food rations which probably aren't all that, all of which made it increasingly likely the general would want to take me up to the penthouse point on top of the M.I.S.C. once I flipped open the heavily-locked lid of my briefcase and he saw there was nothing complex in the contents. Afterblie opened her mouth as if to speak. I think I've got her onside.

Bikbratu

Bikbratu's body was sturdy, his shoulders strong, he dressed well for a man of his age, his face and hair were missing. As we were kerbside catching up with chat, several other people of all types walked past with no faces. Some were hand-in-hand with a partner with a face, nobody had half a face, it was all or nothing it seemed, it looked like only over-eighteens, it was off the scale of impossibility, why hadn't I heard of this?

Bikbratu said it's what happens when you get caught lying, or you big something up and it all fucks up, or you can't afford your neighbour's car, or a deal went wrong with you at the helm. It's a very recent introduction by the gods who are literal in their human-centred damnations, he said. An ordinance was published last week. But I was on holiday, I said. I know, Bikbratu replied, how were the Alps, oh fine, fine. You'd better be careful, Bikbratu, I said. It is a shame to see someone of calibre without a face, this would suggest some unacknowledged weakness or perhaps brief losses of rationality. This I expect from the hoi polloi but not from such a man as you.

You're right, Jaxter, said Bikbratu, but I tend to keep out of other people's lives, it's not a competition if one half isn't playing, I don't do the rat-race thing, I'm cool with myself about all sorts of shit. I keep myself to myself, busy, many activities, I enjoy the look of my face in the mirror after a shave. Then, cruel fate, I'm at the racecourse dressed like someone else for the annual company outing and I lose all my money on a dead-cert named Silicon Stab about whom I had high-quality inside information of illegally-boosted hay. I had put the word around solidly for a couple of weeks, everyone, pensioners, married couples, their children and babies, park people, shoppers, I told the lot of them I was going to win a shed-load.

How can a man be so very wrong? said Bikbratu, dabbing where his eyes had been with his sleeve. He then animated himself like a true man of the theatre, and there was much for him to do. Going over third from home in a five-jump race, Silicon Stab, Bikbratu explained, exploded like a moth between clapped hands, he said. There hovered in the air for the briefest of moments in pinprick form the detonated hide of a young stallion, the legs already dust, the jockey, Wing, left scissored over the fence, his slight frame forcefully broken. Don't you see, Bikbratu continued, I was like you, Jaxter, mainly alone, conducting often gainful business from my home and all of a sudden it felt like the whole world was laughing at me, the hardest laughter from those who are as you see me now, faceless – it went chin first, an extraordinary visual. I couldn't help but stare at the not there. By the time I got home, Bikbratu continued, to tell the wife and children we wouldn't eat this week Silicon Stab was gone in its entirety, from hoof to stardust, but they weren't surprised, they'd felt like something along these lines had been coming for an age, my wife said. Only the air where I once had a face startled my youngest when she first saw me, but she is recovering mainly to plan.

I went straight to the bathroom mirror. I'm fairly sure you'll have one too, Bikbratu said. I'd wink at you if I could, he said. It can happen to the least likely people because here in Royy we all have hidden drives and the devil's desire to stand above and look down on everyone. I never knew it until I knew it. Watch yourself, Jaxter, said Bikbratu to me, you've a nice face, it'd be a tragedy for us all if you were to lose it in a moment of madness. I'll do my utmost to keep your wishes intact, I said, looking straight through him before making my excuses and enduring an uncomfortable journey home where I straightway made a phone call pulling out of a deal.

Vyvyian

I was passing Lee's street on my way to the subway when she rounded the same corner. We knew one another through the office but had barely spoken since my arrival there three weeks ago. We apologised for bumping into one another. As I offered the usual form of repentance, I happened to notice that Lee was holding in both hands an arrow-straight banana.

I will not see you at the office today, Vyvyian, she said, I am the Chosen One! and off Lee went down the street raising the banana high above her head like she'd won a golf competition.

I'm always late to work, so I decided to follow Lee's journey. She was stopping people to show them her yellow grail, answering every amazed question with a sense of righteousness, thinking herself suddenly more important than the banana, dropping in on busy shopkeepers, a crowd gathered and a TV camera appeared.

At the centre of this was Lee holding above her head one dead-straight 12" or so greening-into-yellow banana, more dildo than fruit, surrounded outside the pet shop from which the owner suddenly let loose his baby chimp who ran out, climbed up Lee's back and in a trice had peeled and eaten the whole thing. We were astonished, like stags reared up to the headlights. Peeled it and ate it in two bites and nothing whatsoever happened to the monkey.

Van der Hunk

Fanie van der Hunk was a butcher of everyone's highest order. It wasn't simply the expertise he brought to dicing shanks and sides on his bloody block in the impeccable van der Hunk the Butcher's, no, Fanie van der Hunk was also attracting a growing audience to his weekly meat-mindedness phone-in show at his local radio station. When I say local radio station, I mean Fanie's mobile. Fielding calls for 99 Zlils a minute from mainly middle-aged men about the best way to stun cows or decapitate goats, he dispensed to loyal listeners advice on all manner of carnature. He also attracted the occasional attention of vegetarians whom he cut off immediately for breaking guidelines on hate speech. Which goes to show, I believe, he wasn't doing it for the money.

One unbearably humid afternoon in August, Fanie popped the *Back Soon!* sign on van der Hunk the Butcher's electric sliding doors – it had been a good year – and went to sit in his ample refrigerated unit, working the show from his usual phone, with a cardboard speaker, a button to push, and backed by suspended pigs sawn in half. Pity it's radio, he often said to himself, almost aware of the visual qualities of the butcherly backdrop. As the world outside sweltered, a call came through from Beester who introduced himself as a crop farmer from the outlands. Hi, came the cheerful reply, how can van der Hunk the Butcher help you today? Hunk, said Beester, curtly, why don't you include some vegetables in your meat-filled rants, we're not living 100 years ago, if we were I'd have to write to you instead, why not recommend corn to your listeners to accompany your goose lungs or spinach to go with your chicken, sausage, wolf and venison *chou*-encrusted pies? I'm not anti-meat but I am pro veg, said Beester, a little too piously for Fanie's liking. You'd help us croppers a great deal because as you know, he said, these days many people are turning to meat to satisfy their prandial desires. Where once went fields of beetroot and Hollow Crown parsnips, now come hot marmoset sandwiches and roast fox. And by the way, I had your lamb last week and found it underwhelming, you could usefully start with that, Beester concluded.

Maybe Beester caught Fanie at a bad time, though why this should be with him sat in a refrigerator during a heatwave, making decent money from the phone chat with middle-aged men who came to van der Hunk the Butcher's in order to satisfy their protein deficiencies. Fanie's initial instinct was to engage his caller in a focussed dialogue through which he would expand upon the benefits of slaughtering animals. I am – he was going to say – a butcher, it is a brutal job title. But for some reason – a quirk, a freak, a genetic time-bomb –Fanie told his caller he'd won a prize for the most intelligent intervention of the week, and that Beester should come to van der Hunk the Butcher's to collect his trophy.

As people used to say back in the old days, the rest is history. Photographs still hang on the walls of butchers up and down the country. All these years on, there remains plenty of natter about it. Beester wasn't going to be missed by anyone but that's hardly the point. What fascinates today's public is whether meat-mindedness was in some way responsible for Fanie van der Hunk's moment of madness, perhaps a Group 2a carcinogen had rested on his brain for some years only now to exert an insupportable pressure. There are several enquiries due to report any day. But who am I to mention responsibility? They found Fanie and Beester three weeks later. No-one had seen them around. It turned out van der Hunk the Butcher's classy electric doors had shorted into a lockdown, the freezer door clicking itself shut. Van der Hunk was deep inside a block of ice of unusual transparency. He was holding a shining cleaver in his frozen hands and was stuck till thawing with a grin on his face. Beester's two halves were dangling from the ceiling on a meat hook, the gizzards were out and the bloody pink shanks up like a smoking kipper. I can only repeat it's the best place to be in a heatwave. He should have gone for the beef.

Hemtai

The sky was glistening like petrol on water. The downpour brought an immensity of swill. In the barn, Seth Blǧǧd and his brother, Doobie, were readying the combine harvesters for a duel in the muddy fields. Those boys knew a thing or two about rustic entertainment. I'd stopped by the farm with a delivery of alcoholic horse milk and watched excitedly from my one-seater van which boasts dazzling new signage. 'Hemtai's Booze' will let everyone know I'm in it to get people wasted.

The harvesters swept out like steel royalty but were sludge in seconds. Doobie was in front wearing his favourite 'The Geoffreydots!' t-shirt. They've just had a smash hit across the nation with 'Bach and Crach', a very vascular number to my mind, while behind, somewhat awkwardly in his raised seating area, manoeuvring the pulley gears, sat Seth in his sailor suit. The brothers formed a line of two machines mulching their way to the field in order to have a mud-fest of an afternoon. By now the combines looked like vast meat patties. I've had the horse milk. It tastes like piss. The sky was still an open mouth. More rain was predicted. The boys loved it boggy after a few pints.

It took forever for them to arrive at their chosen wine. It always did. They had argued at length about colour and year, but once they decided, it was liquid carnage. It took forever for them to arrive at their chosen corners. It always did. Mud is mud. I started to doze off. There is just about room. A fly kept me awake. I have a certain respect for flies. Through the dripping windscreen I saw the Blǧǧd brothers climb out of their cabs. Oh good, I thought, they're probably going to kick the shit out of each other in a fist fight. I had another swig of the horse milk to focus my attention. More piss, foul but it snaps my eyes into place. I sit up and scrape my head on the roof. If all goes well, Hemtai's Booze will take off, what with the scorpion wine, seagull vodka and Good Boy! Beer for dogs, I'm seizing on a gap in the market to get my people and their pets unconscious and ill for days. I'm thinking four-seater. The boys are up to their waists in sludge trousers.

As they were taking slow heavy steps towards one another - it was all very disappointing so far - lightning began to strike the ground and fat drops of acid rain inundated the landscape. Doobie, his Geoffreydots! t-shirt ruined by nature's swampy wrath, slipped face first into the quaggy mess and disappeared completely. This was more like it. Seth's sailor suit was awash with filth. I opened the windows to stretch my arms. They came back wet as camels' kisses. I'd like a truck but know I must be patient. Seth shouted something that sounded like 'get up you daft cunt', which is what Seth always says after several. He has been banned from everywhere, he can only play on his farm and we have just struck up an arrangement – my first – whereby I bring the half-time tipples.

I was staring a bit blankly through the windscreen truth be known. I'd had better afternoons. Who did I see now, tired of dragging his rock-heavy legs through nature's bitumen, but Seth, collapsing to his knees. Only his head was visible to me. His brother remained out of view. The rain came down in torrents. I could feel my one-seater begin to float so I chucked the horse milk churn out the window, wound up the engine and reversed sharpish on to the concrete road to town. It took a year to re-lay it. A local counsellor was burned. From there, I was watching as Seth Blğğd's neck and cheeks sank down into his grave. His brother was as good as gone, his lungs sumped with filthy clag, what a waste! I drove off to town in the rain to a pie baked by my wife. Her pies are the antidote to boredom. I looked back at the morass in my rear-view and had to ask what lurks in those who seek turbulence in lives free from responsibility?

Panggabean

Panggabean now lived in a very different continent from Royy. The move itself had been seamless; bloody noses and broken market stalls were already a distant memory. Challenged geographically, linguistically, culturally, dietetically, change had never seemed so pronounced. She knew she was taking a risk but it had dawned upon her after reading a book that not to do so was not to live. This became an integral mantra until one day to the surprise of family and friends Panggabean announced to a crowded dinner table that she had taken up a teaching position internationally and would be gone from Royy for two years. She wanted more experience of the world and I'm only getting as much as is going around she said, looking left then right with barely disguised disappointment. The flight was long and then it was over, she was met at the airport and deposited into a home in a gated community.

On her first night in this new world, Panggabean came across a unique and mysterious red button with ideogrammatic instructions set deep into the wall of the master bedroom where she was set to slumber her anxieties away as soon as the pills kicked in. Obviously, and without thinking, she pushed it; who wouldn't? An hour later as she slept in the magnificently proportioned bed there came a continuous ringing from what she learnt upon bolting upright some three minutes in was her doorbell which was shrill. After some groggy internal debate, Panggabean got dressed and went downstairs.

She opened the door to two uniformed men, caps, belts, radios, the lot. Convinced they were the local police, Panggabean began to quiver groggily, a bizarre sight. This was not the world she so eagerly sought. With a flurry of incomprehensible speech, the two men gestured humourlessly towards the ceiling and stood their ground. They then removed their shoes. Panggabean smiled feebly, like the game was up, but hey. They crossed the threshold and began to climb the stairs, their gestures becoming more urgent, their language more fluent, their actions more boisterous and determined. They seemed to know where they were going. One of them, Panggabean noted pointlessly, was wearing odd socks.

They walked straight into her bedroom. This is some bust, Panggabean thought to herself, seeking consolation in the unimaginable. Then the men began to laugh. Not uproariously, but insistently, as you might laugh to feel better when ill, perhaps you are recovering from devastating news. They're not the police, they're my compound security guards, they've reset the red button, it's my panic button, Panggabean thought via a series of pauses because night-time wasn't her best for clarity.

It took you guys an hour to arrive, Panggabean lamented, nodding heavily and throwing her arms towards the ceiling as if she knew all along and had succeeded in duping the locals ninety minutes into her two-year contract. The men left, all humourless laughter and leaping hands. Immersing herself fully in this strange incidence of cultural exchange, seeing this as an opportunity to engage at an early stage with many differences, to catch this brief ebb of liminality and the snap chance to impart upon the locals her lighter side, Panggabean went straight to the button and pressed it again, set her alarm for fifty-five minutes thence, a dictionary ready bedside. Strange the pills never fully kicked in.

Fischer

Müller, Shanice and Lauaki were in a forest at the edge of a field where their husbands were tilling the land. While the children were at school, the three mothers met here every day. They were building a tree-house for the kids and had finally found the perfect specimen, a barrel round old grandpa of an oak, gnarled, clumsy, crusty, easy-to-climb. Immense. There was a large hole in the trunk about twenty feet off the ground, the ascent was easy, the robust branches unbending, and inside which Müller, Shanice and Lauaki worked together five days a week to build the wooden wonder for young generations to come.

That the oak was not buried deep in a forest but at the edge, where their husbands worked the land, meant the women could see their men but the men not so easily the women, who, though inside a large, exciting wood cavern, were, from a distance, blobs in a hole in a tree. Out of love for their four younglings, Müller, Shanice and Lauaki were, in their spare time, gifting them an almost sacred space; they would, no doubt, spend the remainder of their youth getting up to minor mischief in there.

Hammers (both wooden and metal), chisels, 9" nails, gloves, pliers, a number of solid planks and a flask of tea were hauled up with patience and good humour, spirit levels, tape measures, a dust remover, everything was in fine working order. But, said Shanice, the entry hole is too big; kids like to curl around things. You're right there, said Lauaki and immediately reached for some planks and a metal hammer. Müller handled the nails.

It's probably fair to estimate they boarded up about two thirds of the entrance, seems about right, thinking back as I am, watching from behind the next-but-one tree along. Müller gave the frame a good shake and it didn't budge. Let the fairy-tales begin! she cried out, so that the men in the field turned to the source of the sound but saw little. Then she took up all the tools and threw them down to the ground. Another job well done; they'd better like it, she said, crashing the flask of tea.

Unfortunately, none of the three ladies stood the slightest chance of getting through the hole they had left for themselves, and their tools were down below, their children in school, their husbands in the fields, tilling. Müller, Shanice and Lauaki began to call out to the men. Come, help us, we've trapped ourselves inside a tree. We have no means of freeing ourselves because, like everyone, nice people sometimes do really stupid things. Husbands, come, take up the ladders and help us! Why don't you help us, can't you see we are desperate! shouted Lauaki until her voice cracked.

But the menfolk ignored the cries and went on tilling the land until dusk, by which time the women were hoarse with wailing, parched with entreating, collapsed together in a hole inside a tree. The men went to fetch the children from school, took them home and said their mothers had gone out earlier and were not yet back but that they should not worry. The kids seemed fine with this and they had dinner with one seat empty and soon after they went to bed without the usual story.

I felt criminally guilty having spied on people, hiding in trees is so unlike me, that's not the Fischer I know, it's not in our blood and I was so ashamed that I decided I'd done enough and fell to silence. I had no suggestions for the exhausted women.

Zogglestach

Chan, Elias, Leonarda and Lu were playing a game of lawn bowls at the ladies' club on the promenade when I happened by on my way. I greeted them over the hedge which made Leonarda lose her concentration and deliver a bowl which over-biased and stopped some metres from the Jack. The other ladies looked at me and said, Zogglestach, why don't you mind your own business, it's difficult enough as it is to get away from you and you spot us even over a hedge at the ladies' bowls club. I was astonished. I don't understand, I said. What do you mean it's difficult enough to get away from me when I haven't seen any of you in the last year?

Our husbands talk about you every night at dinner, said Elias as Chan made ready her next bowl. You're never not in our kitchens at supper time. It's always Zogglestach this and Zogglestach that and Zogglestach, Zogglestach, Zogglestach till the cows come home, said Lu, which I never understood as a saying because aren't cows always home? Maybe you're confusing me, I said. Oh, no, it's you alright, said Chan, having delivered a perfectly-weighted pearler that won the end for her team. You're the Zogglestach who stops everyone she sees and talks to them because she finds it psychologically impossible to walk past someone she knows without engaging oracularly, said Elias. Evidence *now*, Leonarda came in quickly. Our husbands marvel at how you go about your business of chatting; they wait in the pubs to find out what the latest encounters have been and how stuff ended up. There's always a bit of a frenzy when news breaks that you've stopped and spoken to someone in the street, believe me. And we're sick of it, said Lu. Our men have given up talking to us and instead quote at length conversations you have had with people you know. It is maddening. Go on now, give us some peace, said Chan, lifting her ball up to face height and advancing towards me; an hour without you in our lives, go on.

I got the message and as I was bidding farewell to each of them individually over the hedge, Chan pushed her bowl flush into my nose which stung considerably, it brought tears to my eyes, it bleed profusely. Somewhat dazed but retaining my ability to do the right thing under duress, I thought to myself, *Pick your hill to die on, Zogglestach*, which is something I remember my father telling me all those years ago. So I pulled out my white handkerchief, waved it in the air a little, put it to my nose, whereupon my blood advanced over it like a flooded delta and I moved off down the promenade to where the whack-a-mole machines were.

Schlomo

Some people want to stay out of the light, for example, the dead. Dead and laid out three floors underground in the mortuary where, ironically, everything's on show. The wattage in the strip tubes is through the roof. Cadavers bled dry and swilling with formaldehyde naked on the chrome autopsy tables. The ones with bodies left are pristine in a tinged-with-sadness way. Two corpses are indecipherable. They are patties one might feed a dog. I find it all so debatable. I mean would you die if you saw all that coming? I'm in a mortuary and I wonder what this roomful of former citizens would say having found their first stopping off point in the thereafter to be a roomful of naked people in unerotic poses. They'd be in a lot of pain if they were alive. Perhaps you can tell the whole death thing makes me uneasy. Which is where Trigg the mortician comes in.

I'm three floors underground on a work-share day. Next week Trigg's coming to mine. He can help me sort the office mail and we'll lunch on salt-beef sandwiches. Right now he's wearing a teal-tinted gown, rubber boots and a face mask that makes his head look very small. He's got a length of tube in one hand and a cheese roll in the other. My nose feels full of bleach. McM'loo, who died an hour ago, is laid out, the chest hair that will never see sweat again, the knees that have buckled their last, the small penis. He fell out of a train going top speed. A second train sent his head, arms and legs into different regions, Trigg tells me. He was picked up with trowels. Trigg has managed to stitch something together and I recall when I failed my cub-scout badge for sowing a button and cooking a sausage and how the cub master always kept me back till last.

I don't like being in here, the razor-sharp glare, I feel exposed but I don't want to spoil what Trigg is clearly enjoying, given that he hasn't got the sanest job going. Watch this, Texeuro, he said, and started wheeling the corpses into formations before having a game of five-a-side football with them. The suicide Pendletock scored the winning goal. I wonder if he knows. 'Look, he said, let's put all the heads together in a tight circle, their bodies will fan out like an elaborate arrangement or a doily. He ate his cheese roll in three bites. There was no stopping him. Smeltt the coronary, Bebopps the pedestrian, Xiddle the driver, Ripov from the gun club, Askmè the swimmer, and Claire, who died in childbirth, were briskly transformed into a persuasive geometrical form, like leaves around a daisy whose beaming yellow face had drained away; the greying flesh and chrome combo was decidedly akin to the psychedelic experience I had with Runce in her bedroom last week. I began to count the pores on Trigg's face. It can't be good for you, checked out and emphasised in full amid muted strangers. Stop all this beautifying death nonsense, Trigg, I say, there are only so many patterns possible and anyway if you're really going for some proper quality you should find participants who care.

It must take its toll, living with the dead. But then it must take a certain type. At school, Trigg was very good at art but I remember his frustration with water-based paints, there must be more, sir, he said to Schlomo, our teacher, who told us to pipe down and get on with it the bell's going in ten minutes. I always felt Trigg's frustration but I never told him so. He might think I'm coming onto him. I still don't like it here, my mouth's gone dry and now Trigg is lining them up for a game of chequers but they're all the same dead pale hue so who's going to be on what team is something I do not know. I sense irony. He is clearly a failed artist with gruesome professional responsibilities. I am not comfortable with the crossover and am planning to let him know. I want to tell him that in the old days they used slabs carved from the floor, none of this chrome stuff, and nobody complained. I feel as if the light has stripped me naked. The whole work-share experience has left me leaden. I return to the street above in order to hide again.

Karlsson

Tombalayu was at the market buying ingredients for his restaurant's evening menu when an avocado, which he was gently squeezing, was whipped from his hand by a man named Nssān who was well known in the vicinity for this kind of behaviour. Tombalayu, of calm demeanour, asked for the return of the avocado, which by now, it must be said, had lost its lustre. In return Nssān picked up a fresh cucumber from the box in front of him and hit Tombalayu over the head with it. Don't just stand there, Karlsson, help! he said to me. But I just stood there holding my tomatoes.

Much out of character for Tombalayu, there ensued an unseemly fight between men using vegetables on one another. Until, that is, Tombalayu poked a bunch of garlic into Nssān's eye who fell to the ground in agony, at which point Nssān's friends – a band of ne'er-do-wells – gathered round Tombalayu threatening him with sturdy carrots and pointy broccoli. Honing his skills as a restauranteur, Tombalayu dropped the avocado and fled the scene amid the usual confusion where a mass of vegetables is concerned. It was all very odd to me because this region has some of the finest cucumbers in all Royy.

Tiktako'o

Shy Tiktako'o fancied Robinson, a boy at school so she went to Rǔne the witch doctor for a potion. In one week, he will show great interest in you, in two he will come to your home, please recycle the bottle, said Rǔne waving a stick.

Back in her bedroom, Tiktako'o popped the tiny cork, smelt the briny liquid, swished it round the bottle and necked the lot first go. That tasted like piss, she thought, before wondering whether she'd been rolled over by the shaman to whom, it must be said, fewer people were turning these days. There should be some artificial flavouring, she thought, placing the bottle in the glass collector. Admittedly she had never tasted piss so her simile lacked credibility. She was offered it once. She then pictured Robinson with such intensity it was suddenly school the next day or the next day after that.

Sure enough, seven days in, Robinson appeared at her side one afternoon after games and told her he'd really like to get to know her better because she was so … mysterious … and they should really hang out how about tonight? Tiktako'o's cynicism auto-combusted. This shit's for real, she thought to herself as she sat beside her *nouveau beau* under the stars after a light dinner where they spoke of drugs and alcohol and music and parents and partying and friends and love. What they wanted most was more freedom and later weeknight bedtimes. Robinson said, yeah, man, I'm chill.

The brew was 100% true. Hey-Presto one week later Robinson was indeed on his way over, having picked up Tiktako'o's mother, de Louise, at the mall, they'd not met until sat side-by-side at the hairdresser's, it was lust at first sight, de Louise was a closet-cougar, Robinson a closet-toy-teen and fate had thrown them together in the pursuit of beautiful hair. Even the staff were embarrassed by their obvious come-ons under scissors.

Both permed and dusted down, de Louise swung them home where she and Robinson were going at it like wrecking balls when Tiktako'o walked into her mother's bedroom straight from school wondering what all the din was about.

For me, the jury's still out because Tiktako'o is a born liar denied attention as a toddler I think, and you've glimpsed the mother, we've heard similar stories from her before. After a mild psychosis, Tiktako'o went over to the witch doctor loureto ask for her money back but it was almost as if Rûne knew what was coming and shut up shop, or yurt. I saw her at the job centre last week. She wasn't carrying her stick.

Pinkie

My favourite bench by the wild cherry orchard, countless hours, a whiff of mint, birdsong, there is a burnished silver plaque for Arbrecht Goofla who loved it here. Someone has carved a phallus into the wood, it's definitely top heavy and I think back to when my wife and I first met. I am pale and shaded, yesterday's sun lessons learnt. The sky is, however, burnished and full of clouds like fingers reaching. I should be at work but I'm funny like that. I am completing my sketch of the scene; the light a cerise rash; the cherry trunks oozing sap from cankers into wispy Pampas grass; Doolien crouched down in it spying on me. I think I've caught the shadow round his eyes rather well. Doolien has convinced himself I am a famous singer. I am a welder with amateur artistic tendencies.

Wherever I go I see Doolien tucked up somewhere, secreted, his mission to stare at a famous person. It was Ottmeyersbrig who told me first. Doolien had a photo of me in his locker at work, he said. He's been telling everyone I had three number 1 albums in the last twelve months when my voice is unsteady, my appearance unkempt and my prospects unexciting. I don't know what to do about it. While Doolien's delusion is absurd, he has become part of my life. On a philosophical level, I can't say, but in terms of a strange sense of companionship, he is there for me. We only know one another from the dog-training school. I've seen him lick dog lick off his hand.

His poorly disguised presence over the last days and months has showed me how lonely I must be because I'm basically spying back on Doolien but instead of binoculars I'm using oil paint. I was telling Pinkie this last week but she walked off. I sat at home after welding metal all day thinking how lonely I must be before I remembered that Doolien from the dog-training school was stalking me and I should get out first thing and do the same to him under cover of charcoal and vellum, a respite from the harsh chemistry of my day job. I should be glad of the attention these days I suppose, but I still hunger for another shot at true love.

Doolien has hidden in trees, rubbish bins, prams, pillar boxes, cars, shopping trolleys, parcels, ponds, umbrellas, a dog suit, a turban, chimneys, manholes, my sketching has really come on, my hand steadier than ever, I might even try and sell one. I pick Doolien out in seconds because wherever he hides a bit of his head pokes out which I depict with a smudge of black and now he's in the wispy Pampas grass at the back of the orchard, to me this is an act of love however so twisted, Doolien came to dinner twice when my wife and I were together, she found him irascible, I cooked him rice, he lives alone too. I feel deeply grateful for his current misconception. I am as far away from a famous singer as the lone ant is from the mound. Doolien is not mentally stable. My shoulders are still a bit burnt. I'd like to give him a hug but I don't want to lose him forever. What he doesn't know is he's got the wrong shaped head for hiding outdoors.

Grygor

Grygor appeared like magic from a large leafy bush with Panton, both looking very happy with themselves. You two look happy, I said. What's up? Oh, nothing, said Panton. That's right, said Grygor. Nothing. For a joke, I threw our car keys in there, he said. That's right, said Panton, we've been scrambling around to find them.

I told them how much I used to love hunting Easter eggs and they smiled at one another and ran briskly into the rising sun. Had I only come ten minutes earlier I might have helped them, I thought, finding another empty bench to enjoy the day warming up and a chance to slide my boots off again. Ah, the smell of fresh cut grass.

Cid

The gallery was awash in oil, neatly framed canvases lined every wall depicting two-story houses with burgundy tiled roofs, curtained windows, spotless lawns, picket fences and wicket gates, the sun an ocra orb in the cloudless sky-blue sky, families gesturing their stick arms outwards. The exhibition had opened at last. There were also watercolours of sausage dogs, lilies with a single fallen leaf, sparkling fruit bowls and portraits that looked just like photographs with dabs of colourful acrylic on them. The place was half empty.

A private viewing is the perfect forum to debate the worthiness of art in troubled times, is it simply a distraction, said the curator Geltonęs to the meagre gathering of wannabe power players who were all looking elsewhere, or can we locate in the depths of artistic endeavour the answers to the pressing questions of the day? Though I had plenty to say on the matter the tranquilisers had made my lungs heavy, but basically I would have slurred something about how the painters had tried their best. Geltonęs had a picture book out and it was rubbish. She signed mine merely 'to Cid from Geltonęs'. I wish I'd never met her.

Geltonęs, here's a pressing question for you, said Demonstralecht the banker in a power waistcoat, there's one word for this stuff and it's shit, would you agree, my Siamese could do better and she's got a leg missing? Geltonęs was ready, Demonstralecht did this every year, it was a classic case of big money butting its way into the creative world, or industries. I thought about the poor-quality seascapes I saw on Demonstralecht's wall when he turned me down for the loan, he could afford so much better but his taste is in his arse. There's previous. Geltonęs knew her terrain. Forewarned is forearmed she thought, taking a long breath and looking Demonstralecht clear in the eye. What's your cat's name, she said? Tripod, said Demonstralecht, by way of a reply.

Glenda

When she was a teenager, Glenda used to drive her dad's sumptuous truck while he slept in the back. They hopped continents on roads. Umberbum tutored her for this specific purpose, having suddenly and inexplicably decided to spend the rest of his days spread across the rear seat of his prized possession while his daughter pumped serious gas from coast to coast, S to XXXXXL, up through Morereason County, down to Fooktown, Texle, somewhere in Spattle right there on the border. Ha! Royy's place names are plain laughable.

Few lead, most follow, Umberbum thought to himself over and over as he lay curled into the plush leather linings he'd had laid down for this, his retirement. He never thought to ask Glenda whether she missed her mother or her school friends or her dog or her brother and Glenda never thought to offer much in return so they sped from highway to highway sometimes for weeks in silence and got to know one another far better than many fathers and daughters could ever manage.

These were the early days of connectivity and Glenda and her horizontal dad quickly became celebrities because they were the first to think of it. Umberbum's obsession with staring at the ceiling of his truck until he died, and the daughter's unquestioning loyalty, her ease with the camera, and a possibly-forged driver's licence that the police were of no mind to investigate, all conspired to net them millions of followers who were desperate for people they could follow.

Finances were thereby secured. Everywhere Glenda stopped people came out to see The Back-Seat Guy, in winter through closed windows, in summer sometimes when the warmth was right he'd roll one down with his toes to introduce himself to the crowds that massed around this prophet-of-the-quiet-life. They always left alms for him, which went towards a new blanket the first year and a valet service that went badly wrong the second.

After he died, Glenda had his corpse embalmed by the friend of a fan and returned to the back seat, to the position in which Umberbum passed his last breath. He was only 35, this was when Glenda was 17 and she drove him alive for a good 18 months. She's still going today, occasionally she stops off during her zig-zag dead-dad mission, we drink some beer and she takes me out to see the corpse, he's in immaculate condition. He makes me think of Young Lenin if he had been buried on the back-seat of a truck with a mile-wide smile up to his glittering eyes, it absolutely stinks in there, I don't know how I am going to tell her. She is clearly habituated to this unusual life-style choice but she's 23 now and has seen more gas stations than there are stars. His death certificate gives 'failure' as the reason for death and let's face it, he used to defecate into a bucket and piss into a pot from where he lay.

Lisaleth

Lisaleth inherited an animal-centred theme park from an uncle in Gijana. She'd never much thought about any of those things and suddenly they came at once. The condition of the will was simply that the park not be sold without a good go being given to its survival now Uncle Verkyl has passed on. Lisaleth sat open-mouthed in the lawyer's office. Gijana, she said mostly as a question, but it's on the other side of the world.

No, replied Stem, her lawyer, it's just out of town, towards the northside, you know the one, *Roarville*, no, you've never been one for that kind of thing, have you? Your uncle means less to you than you to him, it's plain. Quite what Stem was alluding to given this was the one and only time they met is completely beyond me; no less than Hawking-esque in its density. I am amazed Lisaleth thought nothing more of it. Instead, she gathered her energies for success.

Lisaleth flew into the management of *Roarville* like a bird cheating a turbine. Within days she'd held several senior level meetings, it was agreed to change the name to *The Wild and the Wet!* and had parted ways with anyone who'd worked there for more than two years, she had read Mao at college and was taken by permanent chaos. Next she imported real animals from all over the world to fill the empty cages, to do what is at least a minimum for an animal theme park and have some stuff alive. She also introduced a conservation program for local worms which are the only continental members of the phylum *Annelida* to glow in the day.

Finally, she painted the whole area a fresh jungle green with her own brush and installed piped music appropriate to the new Killers! pavilion in which she had found all the snakes to be dead and thrown into one tank that looked like a square blender full of snakes. Lisaleth could smell the rancid flesh through the glass and she was ashamed of her Uncle Verkyl for his mistreatment of the animals.

I'm happy he died, she thought, adjusting her industrial mask and removing the snake soup slop by slop. Lisaleth was amazing, all her new employees agreed.

.The day the animals were delivered everyone dressed smartly as if greeting royalty instead of wild jackals and frogs. As the various cages, boxes, cases and Tupperware tubs were lead through to their new homes, the lion, in a moment of high-density drama, broke clear of his bars. There was pandemonium and the beast, hungry enough, always hungry enough, was about to leap on to Bekilay, the number two in the organisation, when Lisaleth came calmly between them. And she made the lion lie down before her.

Whatever you want to call that, my big question, now that Verkyl's snakes have been slopped out, is will there be any damage done to animals in *The Wild and the Wet!* like there obviously was before in *Roarville*. Why am I asking, because I need to kick a goat sometimes and I'm not alone, a lot of us on the production line talk about doing the same, and if the company under Lisaleth doesn't subscribe to such righteous abuse then I'm definitely not going, nor will I recommend it to my colleagues, it costs enough to get in as it is, I've heard the gift shop's physically unavoidable. We all need to kick a goat sometimes when we've argued with our other halves. Just because we live rurally doesn't mean we kick our other halves, there are times we could all kick a goat is what I'm saying. We're so rural there aren't goats.

Getting where I am now has been like leaping Mount Etna and splitting into a thousand spangled pieces, it's understandable I'd like a guarantee: does *The Wild and the Wet!* have, or have plans for, a section where I can kick a goat and will I have to pay more? This goes out to Lisaleth direct because you are not returning my calls. Think hard, Lisaleth, this could be the start of something, a new dawn or communion or coalescence with animals, state-sanctioned, unique. There'd be a Wikki page within a week.

Xāndersőx

Xāndersőx earned on the side from voiceover work, his rich baritone and slight lisp had led to him dubbing some well-known stars and then he'd call local companies on some pretext or other and get sent stuff for free because the staff member thought they were talking to the famous Janks or Hachman or Backson or Jachchan instead of Xāndersőx for whom this was a mere side-hustle. Soon enough, people of all ages began to converge upon his humble abode in the stretched-out part of the southside. There was some debate about why such a megastar should live in a virtual swamp but it was passed off as celebrity eccentricity.

They came from miles around to hear the master mimic a variety of Oscar-winning superstars with his slick propensity for direct sound-a-likes and other subversive and sexy accents. Having travelled mostly by water, the throng knocked at his heavy door but Xāndersőx never answered. The windows had been painted black from the inside and the letter box was taped up.

He was there, waiting for silence, checking his calendar to see who he was that day before dispensing wisdoms or fabricating anecdotes or setting people against one another, all from the base of the chimney which acted as a quality piece of audio equipment. In other words, life continued as usual, Xāndersőx sat amassing words and dust, ate a single poached egg with two bread soldiers three times a day, a touch of white-wine vinegar into the boiling water, the smell of his youth, and there, at the kitchen counter, well, how many thoughts had been conceived on top of that, what labours had come from rolling his favourite tobacco at the kitchen counter while staring blandly out of the window at the distant church cupola that looked like a boil?

I must be grateful for it and for my tobacco dealer even though he is exploiting me because he too is being exploited, thought

Xāndersőx to himself standing at the counter before moving to the chimney and mimicking one of the region's beloved actresses. Poaching eggs takes Xāndersőx back five decades in fact most of the time Xāndersőx is eight which is another good reason for him to remain interred if not speechless.

Mùselmere

Mŭselmere was a busy architect who lived and worked in a studio opposite the tram station on the north side of town. Her building was a four-story school, one whose very genesis lay in Mŭselmere's renown tectonics. Built to order, her studio, on the top deck, had for the last five months, for fascia-cladding purposes, been covered in scaffolding.

To anybody else, the shutting out of light, the interminable dust, the labourers' weed butts on the balcony, the deadline-what-deadline of work's dishonest days, would have been a trial. To Mŭselmere though this came with the territory. I can't claim to be a sky-high-gold-and-diamonds woman without enduring what all my workers endure, she said to no-one. Evening upon evening she sat outside to watch the strangely articulated end of day and saw fewer stars through the iron bars and had come to feel – as I do often – less consequential. But unlike me, Mùselmere let it ride, it couldn't be changed, and it was, let's be fair, her profession.

Winter's darkness, through which the scaffolding yielded only passing headlights in one direction and red brake lights the other, like gangs of tropical fish leaving town after a dust up, had turned to summer's harvest, scalding heat, and long days into night. At 9pm, the sun tipping its hat, Mŭselmere was on the balcony where the light was ample through the scaffolding's straight lines when two trams crashed headlong into one another directly beneath her studio. Cars swerved to a halt hitting people either side of the road and the whole place erupted like The Beatles had just walked in and were not popular amid brooding national resentment that the wrong one had been assassinated.

The cacophony was stupendous if Mŭselmere had an ear for chaos, but she immediately put her hands to the sides of her head and her mouth hit the balcony ledge when she saw through the strict bars the mess which to her resembled germs latching onto one another as observed through many Petri dishes. The technical reality is that Mûselmere was trapped in a Gaudi-through-the-veil-of-Escher nightmare and could barely breathe in a lungful of dust and dander, let alone move. She was frozen to the spot. Apparently, this happens all over the world for different reasons. Emergency vehicles arrived to blast the *tableau vivant et tragique* with more senseless noise.

It was a triple-plus disaster movie down below, as attenuated via deadpan geometry. For Mûselmere this was by far the most serious aesthetic emergency she'd ever faced, bodies were hanging from mangled mechanical masonry, traffic, people, bloodied, everywhere, the swarming dead, not knowing where or why, now following a nothing or a no-one. Many people lay flat like starfish at the busy intersection where the collision had taken place which made Mûselmere want to descend and help but seen thus they were to her more numeric than human and besides her body was frozen on a massive scale by the shock of experiencing this present carnage as filtered through lengthy platforms of steel and brackets. It had taken the right background for the foreground to be called into question, all of it subsumable *en plein air*. Obviously Mûselmere made it because I had a quick chat with her last night but I will say she slurred her words in a way that couldn't have been through drink.

Bereshynkov

Half-way through my walk to the shops it occurred to me I'd left the stove on again. I turned back up the ancient marble steppes and saw Bereshynkov at the top waving to me with his mangled hands. I wasn't in the right footwear to run. I want my five Krongs back, he said, as I climbed awkwardly to a halt next to him. Six months is long enough. I was aggrieved because now my wallet would be empty and I'd have to steal a handbag up the hill again. Never mind. It was a beautiful day with a soft breeze, echoes of children bunking school, and a hint of tomato sauce and marijuana in the air. All right, I said, placing the note in his mangled hand and showing him my empty wallet defiantly. My wife says whenever I try to look defiant it makes her laugh. Not Bereshynkov though, the frowner. There's less to you than meets the eye, Bereshynkov said, looking away, which I thought odd because I was wearing my boots with the big heels.

This wardrobe choice, I suddenly realised, had been a mistake, given the temperature, the thickness of the leather, the mess they make of my feet, and the fact that Bereshynkov had totally ignored them, not even a side glance. It was a strange decision since I was otherwise attired appropriately for the time of year and its climatic realities. I do look good in a vest. I went to sit on a nearby bench to remove the boots for a moment's respite. I stared at my sweaty, swollen socks. What could I have been thinking, I thought? When I looked up Bereshynkov had gone without saying goodbye. Some people are unfathomably curt these days, I thought, twisting the boots back on and stomping down hard on the soles when I stood up tall. Ouch. I was broke and prepared to steal. Whoever it is will have to be really old because I definitely can't run in these.

Quillerdik

Crossing town about three hours ago, I bumped into Hurrdiìgurrd, who looked very agitated. There's been an incident at the glue factory, he said. A disgruntled former employee had entered the area where all the dead animals are fed legs-first into the grinder, he was armed with a bag of celery. All hell broke out, Hurrdiìgurrd said, my son, Very, works there, there's a cordon. What will I do, Quillerdik, he asked, tears forming on the other side of his heavy, industrial glasses, my Very, oh my Very.

Because Hurrdiìgurrd was always agitated, always fussing about something, I chose to remain silent for a moment. We were stood on the corner where the soup kitchen and the soap shop meet, two people exhibiting completely different body language in the repugnant stink. I was staring at Hurrdiìgurrd at the same time as a distressing energy was pouring from his mouth, and I thought to myself, some people need better public speaking skills. Then I stopped listening completely because his cousin, Waca Zeppaldo, with whom I'd had dinner two nights ago, had dropped a bombshell at the end of raspberry ice cream.

Zeppaldo is the world's most famous trigonomotrist, how he's Hurrdiìgurrd's cousin is a complete mystery to me, talk about inverse proportion. Unlike Hurrdiìgurrd's crude geometric shamblings, Zeppaldo is all side lengths and angles. We once played bowls together at the club on the seafront but drifted meaninglessly apart. Out of the blue, Zeppaldo phoned the wrong number, he said, but now you're there, Quillerdik, you might as well come over for a bite. I was happy because these days I don't eat enough.

Our napkins were stained and spread across the table and our beakers emptied when a dreadful silence passed through us. On the opposite side to me, Zeppaldo flicked his eyes in several directions before settling on mine and said, look, man, this is a tricky one, I suppose I'd better ... Just blurt it out, Zeppaldo, I said, yes, said Zeppaldo, pulling the spoon from his mouth for the final time, just blurt it out. He looked at me deeply and excitely, a tiring challenge surely. I felt sated by the average food. I've always thought his eyes were from two different people and I tried not to laugh. Ha, it's been forever. Zeppaldo dropped his spoon in the bowl, pushed his chrome chair back on the parquet, stood up, leant over me, put his left hand to his forehead at a perfect right angle and said, Quillerdik, I've got syphilis. A drip of cerise-coloured ice cream hung on his lower lip. We had chicken for our main, it was rubbery.

Zeppaldo swept out of the kitchen and sat down dramatically at his priceless Ladivarius piano beneath the abstract expressionist garbage he'd never got rid of. He began a sad sonata. I have fallen, Quillerdik, he said, sweeping his tense skinny fingers across the keys, I've had a moment of weakness after thirty years of reasonably happy marriage – his lengths and angles were simply superlative – oh, help me, man, he said to me, I put my chopper inside a heath-bounding rabbit and now I've damned myself to a slow, mad, sexually-transmitted death. At this, he raised his hands high above the keys and brought them down to a sound like an airline catastrophe. I was much more than astonished.

Did I hear you right, Zeppaldo, I said, my face tautening with horror, did you say, I did, said Zeppaldo, interrupting, which is not one of his better traits. A year ago I was having a turn on the heath in a violent storm when about 3am, my wife, Ang, still out with her laughing friends, things have been mounting, I had an overwhelming urge, soaked to the skin, profoundly given over to nature, and part of what rushed out of me in that monstrous open-air nightmare was a spoken desire to put my chopper in something. The rabbit just happened to be passing. I cannot speak of the act itself so don't ask. It was all side lengths and angles. I was not myself, Hurrdiìgurrd, I was someone else, someone with a wild rabbit on the end of his chopper. It thrashed and we consummated. After a month all my hair fell out. What you see now is a mirage. Ang sent me to the spare room. Then I developed swollen lymph nodes, a curious sensation. My doctor took blood, informed me I had tested positive for syphilis and asked me if everything was alright at home. He's not a friend and I was affronted by this line of questioning. But I still had syphilis, so out of the two of us, I was the wrong one. I don't know what I'm going to do, Zeppaldo said, my reputation, man, they must never find out, and he made a frail but beautiful curvature of his arms, at which point I made my excuses and laughed all the way home about his eyes.

There's Hurrdiìgurrd now, restless in my mind's eye, still banging on about his son, Very, and the vegetable lockdown, and throwing his arms about with utter disdain for side lengths and angles and I think to myself, I bet that rabbit will end up legs-first in the grinder, so I don't really understand what Waca Zeppaldo was so bothered about, though I do feel like I've lost a friend, a talented friend. He and I shall not meet again.

Yinkles

The sun's come out after six weeks and I'm pushing a trolley full of dirt. I have a garden, we like our gardens in this corner of Royy, it's more my project or a project I'd like to succeed at but I have no skill in the medium. I'm laying the dirt on the lawn and seeing what happens. I'm here more for the health of my mind than anything else. Lots of things have died. There was a rhododendron tree. I've basically a patch of scrubland attached to the back of the house. Over the fences either side I see joyful expositions of colour and craft but personally I like to keep a close eye on death and where we're all heading.

Corsody's on the doorstep, his face looks like clouds through the frosted glass, I remove my Wellingtons, reach the door, he's in and past me. Slayntya, he says, I need to tell you something, can we go out on your patch? Fine, I say, aware of the advantages of listening to people in the midst of dead nature. I put my Wellingtons back on and feel a nip of resentment at this inconvenience. I must lay down tarpaulin through the house.

As we stood facing one another in the mud, Corsody said I was sat there at bring-dad-to-school day, around a table with a jigsaw puzzle, beakers, and some fancy tech. I nodded to the dad next to me and picked up a corner piece, there wasn't a great turnout, most dads are too busy or away at war, or drinking. Which nipper's yours then, I said, and he said in quite a high pitched voice, I'm sorry, and I said oh, whose dad are you and he said my name's Yakamural, I go to school here. Here, I said, taking in his full face. Er, I'm in 8A he said. But you're at least 30 years old, I said, and likely more. I was tested, he said, yes, that's right he was tested, chipped in the teacher, Yinkles. This reassured me.

But how have you come to be this way, I said, gesturing perhaps too harshly towards his face. At this Corsody gestured harshly towards mine and we both apologized. I was mostly unmoved whereas Yakamural reeled backwards as if avoiding a punch, said Corsody, he was lithe in a way that younger teens generally aren't. We come from the north, Yakamural said, regaining himself confidently, my father, he is a product sales manager for the vegetable consortium, he looks seventy. I have the mind of a thirteen-year-old, he said combatively in response to nothing, which got me thinking. Because I am a thirteen year old, he said, and I noticed the lightest sprig of hair growing under his chin. He's a very clever boy, said Yinkles and the room agreed. He didn't answer my question but that was some time ago. Later that night I lay awake eating cheap ham straight out the packet and pickles from the east. I was chewing away and couldn't shake the thought I'd somehow been deceived.

Mervyn

Mervyn was a big chap, very popular with old ladies of the district whose bags he carried to their homes, and with the youngsters too, whose football matches he refereed, giving freely his full attention to others every Saturday morning. A model, in this town, at last.

In this violent world of ours, big chaps are rarely picked on so they don't know how to fight. It's the little ones who are jostled or skinny-shamed into a devastating blow; look out for them. How it was that Mervyn, Big Mervyn, Popular Mervyn, always found himself, for no reason he could discern, the centre of violent attention, is a total mystery to us all. I think on it and become a baby during an early-months eye-test.

The day Mervyn fell off the kerb and broke his jaw he told me with great difficulty about the night six months previously when he was smashed in the mouth outside the nightclub. He was on his way to get late fish and chips and had for days after felt the sharp sting of the innocent abused. Right then, he said, as I was looking up from the kerb, something numinous lit up my heart, a sense of grace, he said and he broke into the gaze of a soon-to-be martyr.

In my life, for reasons entirely unknown to me, I've been pounded on top of the head, said Mervyn, scratched, kicked, butted, squeezed, nailed, slapped, stretched, stabbed, stapled, poked, pilloried with gloved fists, and bitten, but never smashed, in the mouth, Mervyn said, rubbing his mangled left ear and wincing. There was that feeling in my heart again, though I was not minded to tell him, it would look very queer indeed.

Once home, alone, the door locked twice from the inside, Mervyn thought long and hard for the first time about fatalism versus self-determinism and the literature this dialectic had brought forth down the centuries. He must have got it from me. I do clever. After several ponderous hours, Mervyn concluded that every act of unchecked violence towards him meant there definitely were irrational aspects to everything.

See, it is still a total mystery to Mervyn too. Oh, when I said fell off the kerb I meant was shoved. That's another new one for him to ponder.

Oronooko

Aagadoo bumped into me in the street. It's you, Oronooko, he said. Yes, I replied. He seemed agitated. I didn't know why. Some people are always agitated. Can you help me with a problem, he said? I'd always thought Aagadoo a decent sort, a bit silly sometimes but compassionate with enemies, that sort of thing. Fire away, I said.

From the right pocket of his great-coat, Aagadoo pulled a small unopened dark-glassed medicine bottle about the size of my thumb but with an imposing outsized black top on top. I've been going out of my head trying to open this, he said. I sat at home for hours in some consternation at how to figure it out and I started to feel agitated which made the contents more urgent so I came out hoping I might bump into someone I knew. I'm so happy to see you, Oronooko! Watch this, he said, hands shaking, he turned the top which began to click round and round like the insides of a clock. Don't you see, he said, wide-eyed and clearly exhausted, there is only lateral movement. Aagadoo had tears on his cheeks. There usually is, I replied. So how come more people don't die! he exclaimed, tugging at his hair and kicking the ground.

Thing is, Aagadoo, I explained, you push the lid down with your palm and twist. Simultaneously. He stared at me with the wonder of the young, fitted the lid in his hand, twisted and, hey presto, the top turned slowly upwards and to his obvious delight, with a snap of plastic hoop, detached completely from the bottle. Without pause, Aagadoo tipped his head back, put the bottle straight to his mouth and let around 20 droplets fall to his tongue which reminded me of a party I attended as a student. There was also a tiny tattoo of a symbol under his chin which I'd never had reason to notice. Well I'll be, he said, slowly returning his head to the plane and eventually meeting my eye.

What's the medicine for, I hope you don't mind my asking, I asked without asking. It's a sedative, an odd one sure enough when I'm jumping up and down bashing the bottle top against the wall, though at one point I did sit and listen to the rhythm of the clicking which seemed to calm me a little bit. Then I fell asleep but fitfully. Then I woke up and went straight for the bottle again and when I couldn't stand it a moment more I ran out of the house in utter desperation. What is this safety click thing about anyway, Oronooko, Aagadoo said? Child-proofing, I said, way too sure of myself. Damnation, that works, he said, his eyes softening into the lightest drift, you wouldn't want kids on this stuff. I sat him down on the door step of Danewanda's Dance Studio and waited till he was not doing much at which point I left him thinking there's zero guarantee Aagadoo's going to remember any of this, I'm not going through that again, must avoid.

Epilogue – Zygmunt

For Luke Kennard

Trouble had been brewing for some time. Both halves of the street lay claim to the chain-link fence that stretched straight down the middle. Clans had come together. Bad breath spread ill-feeling.

The enmity went as far back as the opening days of the bloody Hodgson/Oyuunchimeg dispute and the fear was the factional fighting that marred so many lives forever would return to blight the current generation of home owners in the street. Or that the current generation would turn out to be the blighters.

Disappointingly, both sides dug in; each demanded total control over the barrier that separated them. On the one, Takahashi had hung a flag out of her window with a big 'Ours!' written on it, while on the other, Singh and de Vries had persuaded Van von Van and Kipchumba to let them use their apartment's flat roof as a strategic vantage point.

Things are not looking good, Zygmunt, 'Ndrago said to me down at the end of the fence where the crossroads met to various parts of town. Chen has bought a catapult and Turkit at number twenty-three has invested in a BB gun.

Truth is, stuff got out of hand immediately, insults were traded, a stone flew, and both parties rushed to the clanking divide to grab whatever they could of their opponents, to spit at them and call them foul names, for example Ingerglott a privy seat by Chobkovsky, Oouağaloğalu a donkey's fetlock by Garcia. Then Treblesok grabbed a megaphone and shouted 'scum' through the fence links at Pendikles, who also had a megaphone and shouted the same back. Bottles were thrown, followed by bottles with petrol-lit rags. Desai was unfortunate enough to be hit on the head well inside his own lines by a table that Meg and Schoklok were carrying towards the frontier. He was unconscious for two hours and now speaks only in Wolof.

Parts of the fence started to yield to the constant battering both sides were using as their chief weapon of fear, namely shouts and bangs, holes emerged, crossbows came through, Choudhury was struck straight in the heart and fell dead into the arms of Armstrong who dropped him. This was the point of no return. The barrier between sworn enemies which both claimed as their own, was torn down by the men and women of the great continent of Royy who wanted nothing but to destroy everything different on the other side.

Acknowledgements

With bounteous thanks to my early readers, Leanne Connelly, Chryssi Soteriades and Diana Mastrodomenico. As ever, Lew Klaussner, and , as ever, Potter. And endless gratitude to my university colleagues in Rome for your patience and love.

Warblers - Published by *Berfrois*
Järvinen & Zygmunt - Published by *Foliate Oak*
Matunga & Wickramasinghe - Published by *Man in the Street*
Otowongu - Published by *Flash: The International Short-Short Story Magazine*
Hatzumake - Published by *Tuck Magazine*
Fyodor - Published by *New Flash Fiction*
Bikbratu – Published by *Literally Stories*

LAYY OUT YYOUR UNREST

MONSTERS

OUTTA MY HEAD

D.R. Mills

SEA OF INK PRESS

MONSTERS
OUTTA MY HEAD

Cover by Gabrielle Ragusi
Interior book design by Enchanted Ink Publishing

Edited by Ali Mobley at Sea of Ink Press

SEA OF INK PRESS

For my Dad.

I hope they have books up there for you, old man.

D.R. MILLS
PRESENTS . . .